Fable

An Unfortunate Fairy Tale
Book 3

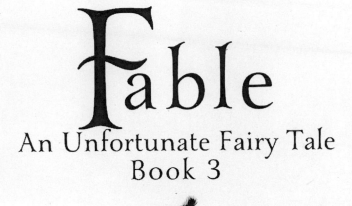

Chanda Hahn

ISBN-13: 978-1491282021
ISBN-10: 1491282029

FABLE
Copyright © 2013 by Chanda Hahn

Cover design by Steve Hahn
Edited by Joy Sillesen
Interior design by Novel Ninjutsu

www.chandahahn.com

To Aiden & Ashley

So that you will grow up loving fairy tales like I did.

One

It was another dog day of summer, and Mina was miserable. The archaic air-conditioning unit in their apartment was on the fritz again, and the small table fan barely made a ripple in the war on humidity. For once, she was anxious for school to start, just so she could be back into the air-conditioned halls, but that wasn't the only reason.

The start of the new school year also meant more opportunities for her to see Brody Carmichael, her long-time crush. Things last year had ended awkwardly when Brody and her best friend Nan Taylor started their almost-dating phase. Or that's what Mina nicknamed "their friend, but more than friend, behavior." Neither one of them was ready to admit they were an item, and Mina was fine with the delay, hoping that both of them would come to their senses.

It was Mina's family curse that had forced Brody and Nan into circumstances that created something out of a fairy tale.

Nan was in a coma and was awakened by Brody's kiss, and since then they'd been awkwardly inseparable. It was as if neither one believed it, but they couldn't argue what fate was pushing them toward. But Mina knew it wasn't fate. She knew it was the Story, or as what she spitefully knew it as — Teague, Jared's brother.

A flicker of movement on the floor made Mina move her head away from the fan to glance at her younger brother. Charlie, oblivious to the heat, was playing some made-up rogue game that combined Candy Land and Clue. Even in the heat, Charlie was still over-dressed, wearing his favorite yellow rain boots, Teenage Mutant Ninja Turtle T-shirt, and a Darth Vader helmet.

He rolled the dice, picked up a double red color card, and moved the little yellow gingerbread man from one game board to the other. Mina didn't understand the game or his made-up rules, but she had a feeling that the yellow gingerbread man did it in the molasses swamp with the candlestick.

"Hey, bucket head, you hungry?" she asked, knowing full well that he could get whatever he wanted from the fridge himself. But she liked talking to him, taking care of him.

Charlie shook his plastic-covered head and continued to scrutinize his boards before rolling to the other side of the board and picking up another character.

"Suit yourself. I'm going up where it's cooler."

Charlie bobbed his head up at Mina, and his little hand waved at her.

Fable

She peeled herself off the living room chair and moved to her room, where she tiptoed over her piles of clothes on the floor and headed for the open window. She clambered over the ledge onto the fire escape and climbed up to her rooftop retreat. It wasn't any cooler on the rooftop, but at least she got a slight breeze. Sweat still trickled on her brow, and she wiped it off with the sleeve of her blue T-shirt. She sat on one of her broken lawn chairs and surveyed the garden of mostly fake plants, a few live ones, and a smattering of eclectic decorations consisting of pink flamingoes, Christmas lights, and a shelf with two gnomes that she had collected at the end of the school year, Sir Nomer and Nomita.

It was the first time in months she had ventured to the rooftop, and she was surprised the rosebush was still blooming. She'd been avoiding the roof ever since her confrontation with Teague, when she had declared that she knew who he was and that killing him would end the curse on her family. He continued to harass her the whole summer, pushing fairy-tale quests her way, but she did something she'd never thought she would do. She ignored them.

She decided to try to take control of her situation…by doing absolutely nothing. Instead of Teague having all the power and making her jump through his hoops of fairy-tale quests, she went purposefully out of her way to avoid them. And it was relatively easy, if she knew what to look for. For example, one day their family was going to the mall, and she felt the beginnings of power stir up around her. A tingling sensation began in her hands and shot up her arms, causing the hair on the back of her neck to stand on end. Mina quickly surveyed the situation and saw the ravens, all seven of them, standing in an odd row along the sidewalk.

She knew it was another test, and instead of being manipulated into a confrontation in front of her family, she exclaimed loudly that they would find better deals at the neighboring outlet mall. Her family got back in the car and left. One after another, she had avoided his manipulations. A Rapunzel quest was avoided by her cutting her hair every day for two weeks. A trip to the zoo turned almost into a disaster when the bears began to talk to her and tell her how yummy they thought she looked; Mina decided that the monkey exhibit would be more entertaining.

On and on her summer went, and she was beginning to enjoy her freedom and the fact that she was, for once in her life, gaining the upper hand, except she was a bit lonely.

Nan had gone off to drama camp and Brody was traveling abroad with his parents, which left Mina alone. Sure, Jared was around, but since she was refusing to attack any fairy-tale business, he seemed to be off enjoying his freedom. He kept checking in on her and would look at her strangely whenever she avoided an obvious quest trigger, but he never pressed her to action. He seemed more relieved than ever at her course of inaction. Plus, he was spending a lot more time with his Fae friend, Ever.

Mina bit back a hint of jealousy and snapped herself out of it real quick. It was thoughts like that which led to trouble, and in her case, the Story had used or spurred on her jealousy to turn her into the evil queen in the Snow White tale. Since then, she'd learned and grown, and had gotten her emotions and power under control.

But that was weeks ago, and Mina knew the Faes' sense of time on the Fae plane was different than on the human one, so it could be any day a gate would open up and a whole army of Reapers could come across, gunning for her—or it could stay closed for years, and she would grow old. Then what? The curse still existed and would pass on to her mute brother or her own children.

No, it would have to end with her. She would eventually have to find a way to destroy the Story. But every time she said those words, she would have to remind herself that the Story was a living, breathing person, and could she bring herself to kill him?

There had to be another answer, another way. She was going to have to stop the Fae and close the gates to their world, and if there wasn't a way to do that, she would have to kill Teague. But what would Jared say? What would he do if she killed his brother?

Music drifted up from the Italian restaurant down the street, and Mina sighed loudly. She would have to make a decision, and soon. Time was running out; summer was almost over, and she felt it in her bones that Teague was going to strike, and strike soon. But when?

She lay back in the lawn chair and closed her eyes, wishing for a sign, for a cool breeze or even rain. The humidity in the air was killing her. She began praying for rain, a hailstorm, even a blizzard, because every second she was getting hotter and hotter.

Maybe she should go back inside. The intense heat on the roof was creating a weird burning-tar smell that made her nose sting. Mina sat up and looked around frantically, sniffing the air and looking at the steam vents across the roof. Black smoke billowed out of them. It wasn't just getting hotter. The building was on fire!

She rushed toward the ledge and looked down at the street below. Their apartment was above the Golden Palace Chinese restaurant, and sure enough, there down below, the Wongs were evacuating guests from their restaurant and out into the street. People began to gather and point up in the air...until Mina realized they were pointing at her on the roof.

Mom! Mina mentally screamed, then recalled she was at work before she remembered Charlie.

"Oh, heaven help me!" Mina cried out to no one in particular as she ran across the rooftop to the fire escape to climb down. Why didn't she hear a fire alarm? She knew the building had one; even her room had one, because she often stared at the red light in the dark when she couldn't sleep.

Black smoke billowed out of Mina's open bedroom window and rose in plumes into the sky. Grabbing the collar of her shirt, she pulled it over her mouth and nose, and ducked into her bedroom. Her door was shut, and Mina carefully felt the door for heat before opening it and rushing into the hall.

"Charlie!" Mina screamed as she raced into the living room. Flames were running up the walls and creeping along the ceiling. His board game was still lying on the floor, the Candy Land pieces scattered everywhere. Tears stung her eyes as she scanned the area for his small form in case he was hiding. She went to his room and found his bed empty. His room didn't have a closet, since it was considered a closet on its own, and she quickly checked under his bed. Nothing!

"Charlie, where are you? Make a noise, hit something if you can hear me!" She was crying now as her heart began to race in fear. Mina ran into her mother's room and cried out when she saw it was as empty as the rest of the house. They didn't own much furniture; there weren't that many places to hide in their small apartment.

Please, oh, please let him have gotten out, she thought. Her only hope now would be that he had run out the door at the first signs of fire. Now the smoke was thicker, and Mina had to crawl along the floor. She tried to head out the front door, but when she opened it, fire filled the landing. Slamming the door, Mina rushed back to her bedroom. The fire hadn't yet reached there yet, but it would soon.

Her hands shook as she flung items off her desk, looking for the key. It had been weeks since she'd locked up the Grimoire, and now she couldn't remember where she had put the key. A loud, piercing shriek erupted close by, making her jump. The shriek came again, this time closer. It sounded like a siren, so she assumed it had to be the fire department.

If Mina was someone who swore, she would have been swearing up a storm at the moment, but instead she tried to think level-headedly for a sixteen-year-old. But in the face of being burned alive, that didn't happen.

She gave up searching for the key and took an aluminum baseball bat that she kept in her room for protection against surprise fairy-tale attacks and began to swing at her desk. It wasn't a sturdy desk, and now that she thought about it, it probably wasn't the best place to store the Grimoire, since after a few hits to the underside of the drawer it came loose. She grabbed the small book and headed for the fire escape.

Normally, she would take the ladder up to the roof, but now she had to get the ladder to release and go down. It was stuck. She tried kicking it and jumping on it, but it only slid down a few feet. It would have to do. She turned and had started to climb down the rungs when she thought she heard someone call her name.

Fable

"Charlie?" She looked up and could have sworn she saw someone walking around up on the roof. The heat was getting intense, and the smoke made her cough. Even knowing it was highly impossible, she felt she had to check. Could she have missed him, and he'd gone onto the roof?

But there it was again, the sound of someone calling. She'd just begun to climb back up the rung when the unthinkable happened. With her added weight, the ladder finally became unstuck and slid down toward the alley. She lost her grip on the rung and fell backward. In a rare moment of déjà vu, she thought she was flying. No—falling. She tried to scream for help, but her words were lost in a rush of air. She saw the sky grow distant as she fell. Arms wrapped around her, and then her world went black.

TWO

A voice spoke through the pounding of her head. "Are you okay, miss?"

"My b-brother." Something was covering her mouth, making it hard to concentrate.

The sirens were echoing between the buildings, making Mina wince in pain.

A young man with "EMT" embroidered on his jacket flashed a small light between her eyes, ignoring her attempts to remove the oxygen mask covering her face.

"Miss, do you know where you are? Do you remember your name?"

Mina looked around and saw that she was a few blocks away from her home, lying on a stretcher. Her eyes tried to focus, but it was now dark, and the yellow blazing fire lit up the night sky, distracting her. Was that her home? It sure looked like it was.

Fable

"Ch-Charlie?"

"Your name's Charlie?" he asked.

"No. Where's my brother? He was in the apartment, and I couldn't find him."

More yelling followed as additional firemen rushed past them, toward the burning building.

"MINA!" A frantic woman pushed past the police tape and darted around the EMTs to run to her daughter. Sara Grime's hair was falling out of her bun; her eyes were puffy and red from crying as she pulled Mina into a hug. "Oh, God! I'm so glad you're okay. I was so worried! When Mei Wong called me and told me, I rushed over here as soon as I could." Sara's words spilled out as she quickly craned her neck back and forth, looking in the other ambulances nearby. "Mina? Where's Charlie?"

"Mom, I…I don't know."

"What do you mean, you don't know? Mina, where's your brother? How could you leave your brother in there?"

Mina started crying harder. "He was there before the fire, and then once it started I went back in and couldn't find him."

Sara dropped Mina's arms and stood stock-still. Her face paled, and she began to shake. Then she turned and ran toward the burning building.

"MOM!" Mina screamed, and tried to get off the stretcher.

11

A policeman caught Sara Grime at the yellow caution tape and held her back as she tried to claw her way to the building, screaming out Charlie's name.

"Ma'am, you can't go in there. It's not safe."

"My boy's in there!" Sara cried. "He can't talk. He could be stuck in there, unable to call for help, and you wouldn't be able to hear him. Do you understand? He can't talk, and he is in there!"

The policeman shook his head in understanding. "The building is about to come down at any second. The fire has done too much damage. It's too late."

"No, no, no! He's in there," she argued.

A small Asian woman emerged from the crowd and wrapped her arms around Sara's shoulders. "Shhhh, shhh, Sara. It's okay." Mrs. Wong tried to comfort her.

"Where is he, Mei? Where's my boy?" Sara crumpled to the street, and Mrs. Wong knelt down with her, whispering and rocking her. Tears covered both women's faces as they watched their home and business go up in smoke.

Mina got up from the stretcher and made her way over to the women. Sara's eyes burned brightly with judgment as she looked at her daughter. "What happened? What did you do?"

"I didn't do anything! I don't even know how the fire started. Do you?" Mina turned to Mrs. Wong.

Fable

Mei Wong shook her head. "No, it came fast, appear out of walls and cover ceiling. Never see the likes before. It was alive. Barely had time to get customers out, before poof! Gone."

Mina stood there, numb; her mind began to play out the possibilities. She turned to look at her apartment building. The firefighters were spraying water through broken windows into what once was their living room. Others were soaking the buildings next to theirs to keep the flames from spreading. A policeman came up to Sara and Mrs. Wong, and they were filing a report on Charlie. He was shaking his head, saying that no one had seen a young boy exit the building. The firemen didn't find anyone other than Mina in the alley, but he would check with the other cars. He pulled out his radio and put a broadcast out for her brother's description, in case he had escaped the fire and was wandering the streets.

She ignored him and walked the perimeter of the yellow caution tape, trying to get a closer look at the building and the fire engulfing it. Charlie had to have gotten out before the fire started. He just had to. Maybe he saw the fire and went to find help? But if that was the case, why didn't he try to warn her before he took off? He had to have left a clue. She couldn't even begin to imagine he was still in there. He would show up. Any minute he would come running out of the crowd with a smile on his face, wearing the stupid Star Wars helmet, and all would be well.

Mina studied the people gathered on the streets. She began to run among them, calling his name. A few people stared at her as if she was crazy, but then she probably looked a wreck. Her brown ponytail had slid sideways and was now on the side of her neck. Her face was smeared with soot, and her brown eyes looked crazed with worry. Yeah, she was a definite picture of madness.

But her brother couldn't have vanished into thin air, could he? A cool wind blew across her skin. Impossible, with all the humidity and the heat from the fire, but blow it did, and with it came an intuitive warning. This wasn't an accident.

A siren call erupted into the night again, and Mina turned to stare at the fire in disbelief. She had heard that sound before when she was in the apartment, and it wasn't the police sirens. She closed her eyes and took a calming breath before purposefully moving closer to the fire. She ducked under the police line and made her way to the alley, where there was less foot traffic. One of the windows had been broken out and smoke still poured out of it into the night sky, but she could see inside the first floor, into the Wongs' restaurant kitchen.

Something was in there. It was large and covered in fire, but it hopped around, floating or flying from place to place. It was hard to distinguish because the color of flame around it was an intense white and gold. She had to continuously blink to even focus on the beast, for now she was certain that it was alive.

Fable

Her eyes hurt from staring at the gold flame, but she couldn't tear her gaze away. There! She saw something—the tip of a flaming wing. Or maybe her mind was playing tricks, but she didn't think so.

A scream ripped through the air, and intense white-gold flames erupted as the roof collapsed into the building. Mina ran away from the building to a safe distance as smoke, dust, and debris rained down from the sky. Something shot out of the building, hidden by the flames, and disappeared into the dark, rolling smoke of the night.

"Did you see that?" Mina shouted, pointing upward, turning to see if anyone else had noticed the apparition. The neighbors and tragedy-gawkers were startled when the roof collapsed, but it seemed as if no one else could see what she saw.

More tears slid silently down her cheek as she watched the fire devour her family's life. Something plastic crunched under her shoe, and she gently lifted her foot to see a partially melted object. As she scooped it up, her heart cried out in despair when she recognized the red gingerbread man from Charlie's board game.

It was still warm, scorched, and its base had melted into a small blob. Collapsing to the sidewalk, Mina stared at the plastic piece and felt her heart break in two. The shock had finally worn off, and all she could do was cry.

Three

The funeral was supposed to be small, consisting of the Wongs, a few of Charlie's teachers, and his friend from up the street. The service was held at a small Methodist church that her family attended infrequently. But the media had made a tragic event story out of Charlie's death and the fire. Signs, flowers, candles, and teddy bears were piled up in a memorial to Charlie, and the pews of the church were filled with strangers, brought together only by the tragedy of a small boy's untimely death.

Mina was numb. Her mind barely functioned, and she had the hardest time completing the simplest tasks, like eating and getting dressed. It was too painful to breathe, and when she did remember to inhale, every breath was complete agony. Sara had always been the strong one—during her husband's funeral, and even now as she held Mina's hand during the eulogy. The pastor was saying very nice things about her brother—what kind of boy he was, who he would have been if he'd had a chance to grow up, and how he was now in the arms of the Lord. The pastor's words brought some comfort, but they did little to erase the guilt that was slowly eating away at Mina. Negligence. That was the word a reporter had used when describing the fire, and how the older sister who was supposed to be babysitting was negligent in her duties.

She stared at the child-size coffin and felt her throat seize up with more guilt and sadness. She had cried all she could and was unable to cry anymore—her tears had dissipated, but the pain hadn't. Someone, probably a choir member, sang a beautiful song about heaven and angels, and Sara was moved to tears. The pastor ended with a prayer. Finally, it was time. The moment she'd been dreading. The burial. Sara and Mina rode with the Wongs behind the hearse as they headed to Gray's Lake Cemetery.

It wasn't a beautiful plot, or a prime spot. It was actually close to the road and near the entrance, but it was all they could afford. Mina thought her brother deserved better, somewhere shaded and maybe with a view, but then again, it wasn't like Charlie was actually in the coffin. His body was never recovered. The flames had burned so hot and so quickly. The firefighters said there wasn't anything left to recover other than the sole of one of Charlie's rain boots, which had been found under the couch. It was then that they had to face the truth—he had died in the fire.

The memories of that night were always close to the surface, like a teakettle about to boil over, ready to send her into a spiral of hurt and pain and loss. They had stayed up all through the night and watched in vain as all the possessions they owned went up in smoke. That same night, the Wongs were taken to the police station, where they filled out paperwork and gave their statements about what had transpired and who could have started the fire. There were some nasty accusations being thrown out about arson to collect insurance on the building, but Mina knew those accusations wouldn't stick.

But that left Sara and Mina alone. Once the blaze was contained, rescue workers asked if they could notify family to come and get them, but that sent Sara Grime into a frenzy.

"No! There's no one. We have no family," Sara answered.

The young man looked saddened. "Well, then, ma'am, let me at least take you to a shelter. They have showers, and you can get a warm meal. I'm sure— "

The slamming of a car door cut the young man off, and Sara looked up in surprise at the white Lexus. Sara's boss, Terry, stepped out of the driver's seat and walked sternly over to Sara.

"Now, Sara, I know that you are going to try and tell me no, but as your boss, I'm telling you that you can't. You're coming home with me."

"Terry, I can't possibly…you can't be serious."

Terry's heart-shaped face and blue eyes peeked out from behind slim jeweled spectacles. Her grayish-white hair was pulled into a severe bun. She wasn't wearing the Happy Maid uniform of khaki pants and polo that Sara and the other employees wore. She was in a gray business skirt, white blouse, and jacket. Expensive rings covered each of her short fingers, displaying evident wealth.

She held up her hand, hushing Sara. "No. Think about it, Sara. I'm your only friend beside Mei Wong. You know that it's either with me or the shelter, and I refuse to let my friend who just lost a family member stay at a place like that."

Sara's mouth opened and closed in shock before she finally nodded her head. She turned to Mina and gestured toward the white car. They had nothing to load into the trunk except for a few blankets people had given them, and of course the Grimoire.

Terry Goodmother lived on the top floor of a large, expensive apartment building. Everything in the condo was white: the carpet, furniture, walls, even down to the five poodles, each named after an extravagant gemstone. There was Jade, Turq—short for Turquoise—Diamond, Pearl, and Ruby.

Sara slept in Terry's only guestroom, and Mina took to sleeping on the couch. Each morning she woke with a stiff back because Turq and Ruby took it upon themselves to sleep on top of Mina. But the last few days had dragged by. Terry's constant chatter did little to pull them out of their shocked state. Complete strangers came by with boxes of clothes and household supplies to give to the Grime family. Terry was great and organized all of the donations in her living room. It was obvious that soon they would have to find a new place to live. They couldn't continue to survive on the goodness of Sara's boss. But Terry was phenomenal at getting the funeral arrangements handled.

Someone touched her elbow, abruptly bringing her back to the present. Mina blinked in surprise and looked up into the striking face of her crush, Brody Carmichael. He was tanner and his blond hair had turned lighter, evidence of his summer traveling the Mediterranean. The wind whipped his hair around his face, but he ignored the torment of Mother Nature as he looked deeply into her eyes, studying her.

Mina's heart jumped in her chest, and her mind blanked. She hadn't expected any of her classmates to come to the funeral. Even Nan was still out of state and wouldn't make it in time. For Brody Carmichael to be the one to show up tore at her heart. She couldn't believe it—it showed how truly caring and special he was, and now it was making it harder for her to not fall in love with him all over again.

Her eyes began to fill up with tears, and her bottom lip quivered with emotion. She was going to make a fool of herself right in front of him. Brody still hadn't released his grip on her elbow, and when he saw her tears start to build up, his eyes widened in concern, and he pulled her close to his chest.

She was shocked by the show of concern and melted into his warm embrace, because that's what it was. His arms gingerly wrapped around her, and his hand gently cupped the back of her head. She refused to move or breathe, and prayed for this moment to last forever as she tried to imprint it into her memories. She was so distracted by his scent, his strong arms holding her, that she didn't hear him whispering something to her. She tried to lift her head to hear what he was saying, but as soon as she did, he abruptly let go and took a step back.

Disappointed by how quickly he'd released her, she stared at the ground, not ready to look into his gorgeous eyes. She knew what she would see there: pity, not love. Her heart ached for him, and it was probably not reciprocated. *By now, if he isn't already, he should be in love with Nan. I mean, who wouldn't love her? She's beautiful, funny, and quirky.* Mina hoped that the summer months and the distance between them would make the love she held for him wane, but seeing him once again and having him hold her in his arms made everything rush back like a tidal wave all at once. She still very much cared for Brody Carmichael, and every part of her wanted to throw herself into his arms and tell him to never let go of her again. But she didn't; she stood her ground, cleared her throat, and gathered her courage to make eye contact. What she saw there made her doubt her decision.

He was struggling. She could see his inner turmoil, the battle that was being fought within him. He had tears in his eyes, and he swallowed nervously. His hands clenched into fists at his sides, and his knuckles were white with tension. He quickly turned his back to her and ran his hands through his hair in frustration. Mina was too scared to approach him and waited until he turned around again.

When he finally did, he was apologizing.

"I'm sorry. I was out of line." He looked in pain. His eyes begged her forgiveness.

Mina was confused, until she remembered he was with Nan. Then it became clear—he was scared what her friend would think. "It's okay, it was just a hug. I won't tell Nan."

Her words seemed to hurt Brody even more, because he closed his eyes and shook his head. "No, I'm not apologizing for holding you. I won't ever regret that. I'm apologizing for what I said."

Mina's eyes widened, and she mentally began to berate herself for spacing out and not listening to what he'd said when he hugged her. What did he whisper to her? What could he have said that would make him so upset? Could she ask him to repeat it, or would that sound dumb? Maybe he was saying he still had feelings for her? Her mind made up a hundred different things he could have confessed to her. The mystery was killing her so much that she wanted to curl up and die.

"Don't apologize. I feel the same way," she lied, and instantly regretted her choice of words. He looked confused and stared at her like a stranger. Great! she thought. She did it again. Insert foot in mouth.

Brody had stepped back from Mina and was now looking around the graveyard uncomfortably. He'd probably just realized how inappropriate their conversation was, considering their location, and was looking for a quick escape. Mina felt sorry for him and decided to relieve his distress.

"So I guess I'll see you at school, then." Not the most eloquent moment, but it would do.

Brody looked at Mina, and he shuffled his feet uncomfortably. "Yeah, see you then." He turned to leave, but stopped as if he'd forgotten something. He reached into his suit and pulled out a slightly crumpled rose. Heat rose to Mina's cheeks when she realized she was probably the one who'd crushed it when she buried her face in his chest.

He walked over to Charlie's casket and held the rose out awkwardly, as if he couldn't bring himself to release the flower. Instead, he turned to Mina and offered the rose to her. That one action alone created another wave of silent tears. She'd sworn that she couldn't cry anymore, but Brody was proving to be her undoing. Gently, she reached out and took the pathetically smashed flower, and she laughed softly. Charlie would be laughing hysterically if he were here to see the state of the rose. It was at one time a beautiful specimen of a rose, and unlike the ones others had brought and laid on Charlie's casket, this one still had its thorns. It must have come from Brody's own garden. Which made this one even more special.

"Thank you," she whispered.

He nodded to her and walked silently down the hill to his car.

Two men came forward and began to lower the casket into the ground. Brody's rose was still in her hand, and she had a moment of selfishness where she wanted to keep it forever, because it was a gift from him. At the last minute, Mina rushed forward to drop her rose onto the others as the casket finally lowered to the bottom.

A few people stopped to speak with Sara and pay their respects, but Mina couldn't help but stare at the rose that she'd tossed on the casket. As much as she'd wanted to keep it, she had to start breaking the ties between them.

But something was wrong. Unlike the other roses, this one wasn't holding still. It was moving back and forth as if blown by a forceful unseen wind. Incredibly, a gust came by, and the rose shot out of the grave and blew across the grass. Irritated, Mina chased after Brody's rose, trying to stop and pick it up, but it continued its wild journey until it flew under the branches of a shaded willow tree.

Mina stopped and parted the long weeping willow's branches, and could see the rose resting against Jared's black boot. Wait…not Jared—Teague.

Teague reached down to pick up the rose and brought it to his nose to breathe in its scent. His hair was a lighter shade of brown than Jared's, and his eyes were a deep blue, while Jared's were a haunting gray. They both had similar angular jaws and drop-dead-gorgeous looks. Teague once again was dressed in black, and Mina had a mind to joke about whether he was going to a funeral, but he was, so the words died on her lips before she even spoke them.

Instead, she glared at him and held out her hand, demanding the rose without saying a word.

Teague's eyes widened and looked her over, never once dropping his Cheshire Cat smile. "I only came to pay my respects."

"What respect? You don't respect me or my family. Otherwise, your kind never would have cursed us."

"You're wrong—it's always wise to respect your enemies."

"Well, I don't respect you."

"You should, Mina. Do you see what happens when you ignore your duty—when you ignore me?" He pointed to Charlie's grave, and his voice became threatening. "I don't like to be ignored, and now you have one less distraction in your life, so you can focus more of your time on me."

Teague's words confirmed her worst fears. Her actions had led Teague to strike out against her family and kill her brother. Her stomach dropped, bile rose in her throat, and every inch of her was sick with the guilt his words layered on her. It was her fault, and she knew it. But she couldn't show him how weak she was, and how much his words had affected her. She had one more person to protect: her mother, and she would not be negligent again.

"You're not welcome here. So please leave." Mina snatched the rose out of Teague's hand and felt a sting in her palm. She winced in pain but refused to acknowledge it.

Teague reached for her hand, and Mina let him open up her palm to inspect her wound from the thorn. She was still reeling, and her whole body shook with anger. Teague leaned forward and blew on the small cut in her palm, and it healed itself. She ripped her hand from his grasp and took two steps away from him, almost falling on the ground. She needed to keep better control of herself. She needed Jared.

"How is my dear brother?" he asked, as if reading her mind.

"Why don't you ask him yourself?"

His eyes darkened. "We are not exactly on speaking terms."

"It wouldn't have anything to do with the fact that you keep trying to kill me, would it?"

"Now, sweet Mina, our fight goes back long before you were born. But you can't hold it against me that I'm only doing my job. I'm supposed to throw quests your way, and you are supposed to try to stop me. It's as simple as that. I can't help it if we have a casualty or so in the process. That's what makes the stories so good." He smirked. "That's what makes them popular. That's what makes me powerful." He was so close to her now that he ran the back of his finger across her cheek, and she flinched and smacked it away.

"I see that you are as disgusting as ever."

Fable

"I see that you're getting your fight back. You know, Mina, out of all the Grimms over the years who died at the hands of my fables, you are by far my favorite to toy with. I wonder why that is?" he asked, appearing to ponder the question.

"Maybe because you picked the wrong girl to mess with."

"I don't think so. I've finally found the perfect Grimm. I think you will be the most challenging. Which means your ending, the tale that finishes you off, will make us both famous."

Mina's lip trembled, and she steeled herself to not show fear. She stood her ground and looked Teague right in the eye. "A thousand sweet words can never disguise the rattle of a viper about to strike. I will not drop my guard ever again. And I will end this curse...by doing whatever...or killing whoever...I have to."

Teague's face turned furious, and his lips pressed into an angry thin line.

"Then be prepared, my dear Mina, for you won't be able to ignore this next tale. I've made sure of that." He stepped away from her. A crack of thunder rattled the earth and she jumped, turning in surprise. A second later, pouring rain followed, soaking everyone within minutes. Mina turned back toward Teague, but he was gone.

Four

Mina ran back to the burial site and gently tossed Brody's rose onto the others. She looked upon the grave and felt her heart rip open anew. Charlie was so young, and none of this was fair: the curse, the constant moving, not having a normal life…all because of their last name.

She ignored the pouring rain and was actually reveling in its cool touch. The rain hid her tears, and she felt as if it was washing away her guilt, her past. She shuddered and made a vow to herself and her brother. "I failed you, Charlie. I failed to protect you from the curse. I'm so sorry. But I won't let it take another Grimm. The curse ends with me, I promise."

Mina heard her mother call her name, and she looked up and started running for the Wongs' car.

It was time to go…but go where? She didn't think she could go back to living with Terry for much longer. But they didn't have to, because Terry pulled up right then with a large white van with the Happy Maids logo on the side.

"Yoo-hoo, Sara! Over here, darling!" Terry waved out the window, ignorant of the rain and the funeral that she'd missed. "I've got the most glorious news, so grab your things and hop in."

Sara spoke a few words to the Wongs, grabbed her purse out of the back of their car, and opened the front passenger seat of the Happy Maids van. Mina followed suit and opened the sliding door, only to be greeted by all their stuff. Or at least, all the boxes of donated stuff that had been piling up in Terry's living room.

"What's going on, Terry? Why did you move all of our stuff here?" Sara asked, confused. It was obvious from her expression that she was a little offended that they were being packed up and shuffled off without any notice.

"Shhh, I can't ruin the surprise yet. Just wait." Terry waved her hands in the air and directed Mina to a small flip-down seat with an old belt buckle. She strapped herself in and felt odd when she looked at the boxes of food, clothing, and essentials piled in the back. It was like they were being uprooted all over again. She secretly wondered if Terry was going to slow down around a curve and push them out of the moving vehicle.

Mina turned to look out the window one last time as they passed Charlie's grave and saw a lone figure standing by the grave, wearing a top hat. Mina craned her neck to see if she

29

recognized the man, who seemed ignorant of the coming downpour. The man with the tall hat was more interested in watching them leave than paying his respects to her brother.

"Mom." Mina pointed out the windows, which were quickly fogging up with heat. "Do you know that person?"

Sara looked in the direction she was pointing, but by the time she turned in her seat, the man in the rain was gone. "What person, Mina?"

"Never mind. I just thought I saw someone."

Mina settled into her seat and listened to the quiet chatter of the women in front and the annoying screeching noise the old windshield wipers made against the glass. Bored, Mina began to inspect the boxes of their belongings and gasped when she saw a bag with her bathroom items in it and the Grimoire thrown in haphazardly on top. She was angry. How dare this woman touch her things and treat them with so much disrespect? Mina didn't care what stupid surprise Terry had in store. Touching a teenager's things was just not done. It was taboo. A giant no-no.

Terry drove away from the cemetery and onto a turnpike. It felt surreal—they had just buried her brother, and now they were getting evicted by their friend and moving on the same day. Mina began to wonder if her mother's boss had a screw loose. After what felt like hours, but in reality probably was only few minutes, they exited the highway and turned down an unfamiliar road. They must be on the edge of town, because she didn't recognize the terrain.

Fable

They turned onto a barely discernable road, and Mina wondered if Terry knew where they were going. Finally, they followed the road up a winding hill, and Mina could see a house in the distance, a very large house. Terry pulled up to a wrought-iron gate, and stepped down from the van and fished around in her wallet for a key card. Finally, she found the right one and slipped it into the security box, and the gate opened. She slid back into the car and drove up the driveway, lined with weeping willows, and stopped in front of a large estate.

It was antiquated and hauntingly beautiful at the same time, as if the architect couldn't decide which era to design the house after, so he merged all of them. Or, better yet, as if the house had been there for centuries, and each century something modern was added to it. It was in need of quite a bit of work and a coat of paint. The outside shutters had fallen off and needed to be fixed, the bushes were overgrown, and the front steps were missing a board. A large greenhouse was attached to the house, and even from this distance she could see that quite a few of the glass windows were shattered and overrun with foliage.

"Welcome home!" Terry chimed happily as she put the van into park. "I made a few phone calls and pulled a few strings, but it's yours."

"What is?" Sara asked.

"Why, the house, of course! It's one of the estates that my company has had a contract with…well, forever. It has sat empty for most of those years, and the owners have no desire to sell it and are hardly ever here, either. So it continues to sit empty, which isn't good for a house. I contacted them and explained your situation and that you were one of my most trusted employees and a dear friend, and they offered it to you and your daughter…on one condition."

Sara looked at the large house, her hand jumping to her heart in fear and wonder.

"You will have to live in it and take care of it. I can recommend a great handyman to help fix up the place, and soon it will be as good as new." Terry's head bobbed in excitement. "Don't get me wrong, I love having you two live with me, but it's about time for you to start anew. Especially since Mina has to go back to school in a few days—"

Terry continued to relay her news to a shocked Sara and unlocked the front door and walked them into a spacious entrance hall. What the hey? A spiral staircase? The house looked like it had come out of a movie, all right…a horror movie.

Off the entrance hall was a sitting room with a library with a very dusty grand piano, while to the right was a formal dining room. In every room there were obvious blank spots on the wall where pictures had been hung and looked like they had been recently removed, because of a slight, barely noticeable discoloration of the wall. They were all prime locations: above the fireplace, in the library above a desk. Each newly discovered bare spot made Mina irritated. Were these priceless portraits removed because the owners thought they would steal them?

There were multiple wings of rooms to be explored at a later date. They kept going and walked into the largest kitchen she had ever seen. It was a chef's dream, with multiple islands and granite countertops, but things Mina didn't really care about. What she zoned in on first was, of course, the dishwasher.

"It's all very nice, Terry, but I don't know how comfortable I am with this commitment. I've never even met the owners. How do I know that they want us as tenants?"

"Pish-posh." Terry frowned at Sara. Mina had to hold back a grin; she didn't think people spoke like that anymore. "Don't look a gift horse in the mouth. I'm telling you, I pulled a huge favor out of my hat, and I can tell you there's not going to be another offer out there like this. I did this for you because I think of you like my own daughter. And you deserve this."

Just then a weird buzzing sound came from a square box in the kitchen. Terry ran forward and pushed a button. "Yes, who's there?"

"It's meee. We bring Sara's car like you asked. Now push button and let us in." It was Mrs. Wong. Terry rolled her eyes before she pushed the button. Mina assumed the big iron gates at the end of the drive were opening. A few minutes later the Wongs entered through the front door, carrying boxes from the Happy Maids van.

33

"Eh, nice big house you get, Terry. What ex-husband did you get this from? Maybe you can give him my number." Mrs. Wong's broken English made her attempts at being funny sound awkward.

Mei's husband placed his hand over his heart with dramatic flair. "Oh, Mei, you wound me. Now stop yammering, and let's help them settle in."

With only a few more failed attempts to talk themselves out of the house, Sara finally gave in and helped haul the last cardboard boxes into the foyer. The Wongs and Terry tried to keep some light chitchat going, but it was obvious from the rings under Sara's eyes that it was time for them to go. Once everyone was gone, the house was eerily empty.

Sara stared at one of the blank walls covered in striped wallpaper in puzzlement. "This house. There's something about this house." She reached out a hand to touch the wall and then shook her head as if to clear the troubled thought from her mind. "I'm sorry, honey, I'm exhausted. Let's find a room and unpack and talk tomorrow. It's been—" she started to sniffle but held it back, "—a long day."

Mina agreed. Was the funeral only a few hours ago? The rain was still coming down outside, and the occasional lightning illuminated the night sky. The second floor was filled with more turns, wings, and darkened rooms. Sara found a room to her liking and settled in by immediately crawling onto the bed and not moving. Not wanting to leave her mother alone, especially tonight, Mina crawled onto the large king-size bed and lay next to her mom.

Sara's eyes were shut, and Mina could see the barest glimmer of tears sliding out of the corners. Her mother's long hair had fallen out of its bun, and a hint of gray could be seen mixed in with the brown. Had this tragedy aged her mother years in only a few days? Mina took a deep breath and quivered with pain and sadness. She slid her hand into Sara's hand and squeezed gently, comforting her mother without words. Sara's breathing evened out, and she squeezed her daughter's hand back. A few minutes later, they were both asleep.

Five

A thudding noise woke Mina in the middle of the night. She sat straight up in bed and looked around the darkened room in fear. Nothing stirred, and nothing moved. The rain still poured outside, and the night sky lit up, followed by the delayed sound of thunder. The brief flash of light proved that nothing was in their room.

She turned to look at her mom, who was still curled up in a fetal position and was sleeping very deeply. She knew that Sara had been worrying about their lack of housing situation, and now she looked like she could sleep for days. Mina lay back in bed and stared at the ceiling, then the walls. She rolled over and tried to sleep on her stomach, but it was no use; she was wide awake. Her mind kept trying to catalog all the possibilities of what could have made the noise, and her paranoid teenage brain wasn't going to let her go back to sleep until she found out what it was. She was still fully dressed, so she tiptoed out of the room and closed the door with a soft click.

The hallway had never looked more foreboding than it did in the middle of the night during a thunderstorm. Mina didn't care who owned the place or what the utilities would cost; she was going to bring light to the darkened mansion. She felt along the walls until she found a light switch and clicked it on. The electric candelabras on the wall flickered on, and nothing jumped out at her.

Phew, she thought, *one down, only a hundred more to go.*

She turned the corner in the wing and was once again greeted with another darkened hallway. She repeated the process and almost panicked when she couldn't find the switch, because it was hidden behind the drapes. When the hallway was illuminated, she didn't move on to the rest of the house. Instead, she decided to tackle every room. How could she sleep if she didn't know what lurked behind each of those ominous doors?

The first door she flung open wildly and jumped back into the hallway, expecting something or someone to jump out, like a bat. It was another empty bedroom. The next door revealed another empty bedroom. The next door—a bathroom. The next door—a game room, complete with foosball and a pool table. She was becoming braver with each door and stopped turning on the lights after the lights in the hallway illuminated the empty rooms.

The second-to-last door was a storage room, filled with extra chairs, tables, fake plants, vases. One section of the room had less clutter, as if all of the offending junk had been pushed away from the central object. It was an easel, and on the easel was a painting covered with a sheet. Leaning against the wall were stacks of what looked like more paintings. Were these the paintings that had been removed from each of the rooms? If so, and they were removed because of fear of theft, then it was stupid for the owners to place all these priceless paintings here in one room. Or maybe they had forgotten to lock the door. Nevertheless, this was what she'd been looking for…answers.

Maybe it was a Monet? Or a Picasso? How cool would it be to actually see one in person? Or what if they were moved into this room so the owners could say that Mina and her mother had stolen the paintings after they'd moved in? She was flooded with a host of different reasons why the owners might have moved the paintings here…and all of them ended up with Mina and her mom in jail.

She had no choice; she was going to have to look at the paintings, and she would start with the one covered on the easel. Just when she was about to remove the sheet, she had the intense feeling that she was being watched. She dropped her hand to stare around the room, and the barest reflection of movement in the glass drew her attention to the large framed window. It was still raining and dark, but she thought she saw something on the lawn when the lighting flashed.

Fable

Being careful to not be seen, she crept to the side of the big window and curtain, and took up a lookout. She held her breath in anticipation and waited until the next burst of lightning. There it was, a quick flash! And sure enough, there was someone in the middle of the yard, staring at the house. It went dark again, and she began to panic. What was that? Who was that? She lay in wait for the next minute until the storm illuminated the yard again.

Boom! The crash was simultaneous with the thunder, and he was there! Right there! Thirty feet from the window, and he was looking right at her. It was the man from the cemetery! He had stopped right outside what looked like a ring of white rocks, and he was beckoning to her.

Mina screamed and crashed backward into the paintings behind her, her fear causing her to subconsciously call for Jared.

An instant later Jared was by her side, steadying her and trying to keep the picture from falling over. "Clumsy, as always. I think you could use another lesson from me."

"There's someone...outside!" she choked out. Her fear paralyzed her, making it hard for her to speak. She pushed him toward the window to look for himself, but he didn't need to.

Jared took one look at her scared face and ran out the door into the hallway, leaving her alone in the darkened room. The silence of the spooky house, mixed with the intruder outside, was too much for her nerves. They were shot. She did the weak thing. She curled up on the ground by the sofa and wrapped her arms around herself, and tried not to fall to pieces. Minutes later Jared appeared in the room with her, soaking wet and out of breath.

"Mina?" Jared called out when he didn't immediately see her.

"Who was it?" she asked from her hiding spot by the couch.

Jared saw her and knelt in front of her, being careful not to touch her.

"I don't know, but they're gone."

Mina shivered. "You believe me, though, right?"

"Of course I do. There was someone out there—I could smell them. I just didn't recognize the scent."

"You mean they were Fae?"

"Most definitely. I just don't know what kind, and that worries me." He stood up and brushed off his knees, and turned as if heading out the door again.

"Wait, Jared, don't leave me." She felt silly at being so scared, but this was real. At first she didn't know who it was and didn't know how to fight it, but now, knowing it was a Fae gave her the knowledge that she could beat it. But she needed the Grimoire; she needed Jared.

He stopped and turned to look at her with an irritated frown. "Oh, so you didn't need me all summer, and now all of a sudden you want me around more? Look around you. You don't need me when you've got all this. Besides, whoever was out there couldn't get past this house's defense, and I doubt that they will tonight, or any other night. Call it a special gift that comes with the house."

"Then how did you get in here?"

"You summoned me, dummy. Where you go, I go. Unless it's the women's bathroom." He made a face at her. "Or you leave the book somewhere really far away or lose it, and then that can cause problems, like you already learned."

"Yeah, I remember," she scoffed. "But what do you mean, 'he couldn't get past the house's defenses'? What defenses?"

Jared moved across the room and plopped down on the dust-covered sofa. A small poof of particles floated into the air before settling around him. He leaned his head back and closed his eyes as if he was taking a nap, purposely ignoring her question.

She stood up and stormed over to him, fully prepared to hit him on the shoulder, when she noticed how tired he looked. His stormy gray eyes were closed in a feigned sleep, and she couldn't help but fixate on his looks. It wasn't apparent at first, but if you looked closely at his angular jaw and the way his skin shimmered, it was quite clear that he wasn't from this world. He was too handsome. His hair was getting a little long and looked like it could use a trim, but it was still messed-up and very stylish. Standing there next to him, she couldn't help but compare him to Brody. The Fae prince could very well take on her high school crush.

She had been avoiding Jared, because seeing him reminded her of her oath to kill his brother. How could she tell him that she needed to become stronger, to work harder, because, *Hey, I want to kill your family.* The truth was, she couldn't. She couldn't face the truth, and therefore she couldn't face Jared.

What could she say? Mina decided to forget it. There was nothing she couldn't tell him tomorrow, in the middle of the day. She had moved away from him to go back to her room when her eye caught the easel and frame that she had almost knocked over. She took a quick glance at Jared and his eyes were still closed, so she moved to the lone picture and raised her hand to pull at the covering.

He spoke without opening his eyes. "I wouldn't do that."

"Why not, Jared?"

"Because some things are best left undiscovered...like Spam. Nasty stuff—that should have remained a mystery." He turned to his side and smiled at her wanly.

Mina wanted to roll her eyes at him, but he stopped her with that haunted look of his. "I'm sorry I wasn't there for you that day."

She tensed up. It wasn't Jared's fault, it was hers, but she secretly wanted to blame him for Charlie's death, for losing their house. But she knew that was a lie. She was to blame. She looked up at Jared and shook her head. "No, I could have called you, and I didn't. It's my fault he's dead...no one else's."

Jared looked uncomfortable. "I was ignoring you because you had been ignoring me. So I purposely tuned out your emotions. I didn't know something was wrong until you fell. I almost didn't get there in time. I didn't know about Char...about what happened till after..."

"You caught me, didn't you?"

He nodded. "I carried you to the alley by the ambulance and left you there. I'm sorry. I was still angry."

"You should have stayed with me. Not left me and my family alone on the worst night of my life. I thought you'd abandoned me."

Jared leapt off the couch and stood within inches of her, his breath warm and sweet upon her face.

"I would never abandon you. I will always be there to catch you when you fall."

She closed her eyes and leaned into him, being careful not to touch him...and careful to shield her heart.

"I'm scared to fall—I'm scared I'm not strong enough for the tasks ahead.

Jared's jaw twitched with emotion. "Then I shall teach you to fly. It's time for you to get some answers. Pull the sheet," he answered.

"You just told me not to."

"Okay, how about this...pull at your own risk."

For once she actually didn't want to know, but he was looking at her with such sorrow in his eyes that she actually was

43

becoming angry at being pitied. She yanked as hard as she could on the sheet, and the easel almost fell over. It settled, and Mina focused on the portrait. A man in his thirties, wearing a brown suit and polka-dot tie, sat on a red lounge chair, facing the artist. His hair was dark brown, and a neatly trimmed mustache framed his nice lips. His eyes were warm and the same boring brown as his hair. It was the same boring brown of Mina's hair. She was staring at a portrait of her father.

Six

"Who painted this?" she gasped.

"One of the Fae. I don't remember which one it was, but it's a pretty good likeness."

"Why is his picture in *this* house?" Mina asked, feeling agitated by this new discovery. "What's it doing here, Jared?"

"Haven't you figured it out yet? The house used to belong to your father, although he never lived here." She stared at him with an utter look of confusion on her face. Jared started chuckling at her. "Okay, now I'm seeing how lacking your training as a Grimm is. Someone should see about that."

"Yeah, why don't you work on that?" Mina quipped back, feeling relieved at finding out the house didn't belong to a serial killer. But it left way more questions that dealt with her father and his death. She wasn't really ready to delve into that, so she let the plaguing questions drop.

Jared wiped away the tears and sat up straight. "I'm sorry, I shouldn't be laughing at you—I just thought you would have been smarter than that."

Mina was insulted and punched Jared playfully in his arm. "I would be if you weren't a deceitful, pigheaded prince who plays both sides of the tales and obviously gets enjoyment out of terrorizing me."

"I like terrorizing you. Your face turns the prettiest of colors." Jared playfully punched Mina back. In retaliation, she pushed him a little harder. Being a boy, and spurred on by the challenge of a wrestling fight, Jared whooped loudly and lunged for Mina, knocking her onto the couch. She squealed and started hitting Jared when he began to tickle her sides.

"Stop...stop...NOO!" she screamed. He laughed and continued his ambush. She tried desperately to catch her breath. She kicked at his legs and tried to push him off, but all it did was bring his face that much closer to hers, and his eyes widened when he realized it as well. He stopped tickling her, his hands on her hips, and he leaned down and nuzzled her cheek. Mina immediately froze and sucked in her breath. Jared stopped and lifted his head to stare at the door.

A second later, the storage room door opened and the light flicked·on, illuminating the room. Surprised, Mina flew off the couch, and something hard fell to the floor. Sara stood in the doorway with a fire poker held out in front of her. Her chest was heaving from running. Her eyes flew to Mina.

Fable

"Are you okay?" Sara asked. "I heard screaming."

Mina stared hard at the plastic mannequin on the floor that moments ago had been Jared. Her cheeks flushed, and she shook her head. "Yes, I was exploring in the dark and knocked this over. It scared me at first."

Sara looked around the room, unconvinced. Her eyes scanned every inch of the room before she nodded. "Okay, then. Let's get out of here. There seems to be a lot of breakable items in here. Is that dummy okay? It's not broken, is it?"

Mina tried not to laugh as she stood up and gently kicked the mannequin. "This old thing? Nah, it's not broken. It's as hard as a rock…see?" She took pleasure in knocking her foot into it one more time, a little harder.

"What an odd thing to be in a house. It almost looks alive."

Mina couldn't help it—she snorted. "No, it's a dummy all right. No heart and all." She walked over to her mom and ushered her into the hall.

"Aren't you going to pick it up?" Sara asked.

Mina grinned. "Nope. It can stay on the cold floor all night, for all I care. It's punishment for attacking me."

"I'm really starting to not like this house. It feels too…mysterious."

"I think it's perfect. It was meant for us." With that, Mina flicked off the light and closed the door.

Seven

"You know you don't have to go today. I can call the office and get you excused," Sara said softly. Usually at this time of the day Sara would be dropping Charlie off at his school, and Mina would be arriving on her bike. But since Charlie and the bike were no more, it was time for a different tradition.

Mina chewed on the inside of her cheek and stared at the school. Just two weeks ago she was dying to go back; now she was dreading walking through the double doors. And she couldn't figure out why. Nan was in there. She would get to speak to Nan for the first time since she left for the summer, but also Brody would be in there, along with Ever.

But Nan may not know about Charlie. Mina had intended to call her as soon as she got back from camp, but it was the oddest thing. The house they were staying at didn't have a telephone, or a TV. Once she walked in the school doors, every student's eyes would be on her and they would pity her, and Mina would probably break down and cry.

What to do? What to do? She was about to tell her mom to turn around and drive home when she felt her backpack grow warm on her lap. A tingling sensation spread out along her leg, and she gripped the car door and jumped out in record time.

It wasn't a mystery what the sensation was—it was the Grimoire, which meant it was Jared telling her to get going. Sure enough, when she had walked twenty feet from the car, he joined her out of nowhere.

He silently walked next to her and only bobbed his head in a casual greeting. Mina tried to smile back, but it was forced. She could feel the tears building, and she desperately tried to hold them at bay. She reached for the entry door and began to open it, but Jared put his hand on the glass, gently closing it. Students mumbled at the traffic jam they were causing and walked around them, using one of the other doors. Jared turned and looked at her, his dark gray eyes filled with emotion.

"Hey," he said, gently touching her shoulder so she would look up at him. "You'll get through this. If today is too much for you, just say the word, and I'll get you out of here. You got it?"

She dropped her head to look at her shoes and found it impossible to swallow the lump forming in her throat. "You promise?"

"I promise. Just say my name, and I'll take you away."

Mina nodded and adjusted her backpack over her shoulder. It now felt like someone had loaded it with bricks. Jared opened the door and motioned for her to enter first.

The school smelled the same, a weird mixture of books, paint, and sneakers. The air-conditioned air hit her as soon as she walked in, and she balked at the memory and guilt that assailed her. Jared gently touched her elbow and pushed her forward. She reached into her green jacket and pulled out a crumpled-up class schedule labeled *Grime, Wilhelmina—Junior. Class A.* Other than her name, she couldn't make out where her first class was located. Her eyes were watering. She didn't even know if Nan was in any of her classes. She was a wreck.

A cute girl with a pleated skirt, black boots, and a skull shirt popped up next to them and latched onto Jared's arm. Her short black hair had a new stripe of purple added to it, giving Ever added flair.

She started chatting nonstop, and Mina could feel the slight breeze created from her invisible wings. Ever was Fae, like Jared. A pixie, to be exact, who had the biggest crush on the banished royal prince.

"Oh, did you see who I got for history—snooze fest. And advanced physics. Yikes! I think I'm doomed to be a student here forever. I'll never pass those classes." The pixie kept chatting until she noticed someone to the left of Jared. When she saw Mina, she paused long enough to say, "Hey, Gimp."

And then she was back to her self-absorbed universe, asking Jared to hang out after school.

Mina shouldn't have been surprised at Ever's reaction. Pixies tended to have short attention spans. But Jared was put off by Ever's words. He pulled his arm out of her grasp and gave her an ugly glare to be quiet. She took his cue and immediately stopped speaking, and slowed to walk a few feet behind them. Jared directed Mina to her home room class and stopped outside the door.

"Here you are, safe and sound," he said lightly. "Don't worry—if you get through today, tomorrow will be a breeze. I'll see you in forty-five minutes, and I'll come make sure you don't get lost on the way to second period. Here, give me your backpack, and I'll put it in your locker for you."

"Wait, how do you know where my locker is, and how do you know the combination?"

He smiled crookedly at her, and for the first time since the fire she felt a stirring of emotion other than sadness. Her mind flickered back to their encounter in the storage room, and her cheeks flushed. It was like her frozen heart had started to thaw just a little at his smile.

"Ah, that's for me to know and you not to find out." He opened up her backpack, pulled out a spiral notebook and pen, and handed them to Mina before turning and leaving.

Mina almost dropped the notebook and had to maneuver quickly to grab it. Instead of sitting near the front of the room, she headed for the farthest corner of the room and sat in the back row. Ever happened to be in the same home room as Mina and gave her a worried frown before sitting up a few rows and over. It was obvious that Ever was upset at Jared's treatment and was going to take it out on Mina.

Students began to file in, and Mina stared at the spiral notebook, preferring to not make eye contact. She must have stared at the notebook for two minutes before she noticed something odd about it. It was the Grimoire, but it was once again in a notebook shape and not the small leather book she had seen it in before. Jared must have changed its shape while it was in the backpack on purpose, then handed it to her. She didn't even know that was possible, but then she realized again—stupidly—how closely they were connected.

She flipped open the notebook and perused through all of its prisoners, because that was what the book was, a jail of sorts. But the oddest of all was how this all started. Mina's ancestors, Joseph and Wilhelm Grimm, had found a way over to the Fae plane and demanded that the gates between the worlds be closed. The Fae agreed, but only if the brothers could complete a list of quests, which would be logged into a powerful book that resided in the Fae world. Unfortunately, the Grimm Brothers had been tricked by the Fae. There wasn't an end to the quests, because if one Grimm failed, the responsibility passed on to the next son. And the challenges started all over again. Mina had figured out that it had nothing to do with the quests and everything to do with being manipulated by the Story. The Story wanted the Grimms to trap the uncontrollable power-hungry Fae that lived on the human plane for them.

But somewhere along the line, a witch or powerful Fae split the Fae book in two and ensnared the royal brothers Teague and Jared as servants to these books, one on the human plane to help the Grimms, while the other resided on the Fae plane. Mina had yet to find out what it was that the brothers had done to deserve their fate, but Jared refused to talk about it. He would only say that he had been banished from his home and must live as a servant to the Grimms. That was how Mina figured out that Teague was also bound somehow as well.

She fingered the pages and traced the faint outlines of the pictures drawn on the paper. There was a lifelike drawing of Claire and Grey Tail, the Chicago Bears football players, and others. Her hand started to shake when she saw the scared faces of the innocents trapped within as well. For a Reaper, a killer that hunts down Grimms, had gotten ahold of the Grimoire and was using it to trap innocent Fae within its pages. There was her teacher Mrs. Porter, a UPS worker, a young girl. Quickly, she flipped the pages and saw Diedre and the Reaper locked in a death grip frozen on the page. She turned one more page, and her heart felt like it was being ripped out. The picture was of Brody kissing Nan, and in the background was the hospital on fire. It was a Snow White and Sleeping Beauty tale wrapped into one, complete with fiery dragon and glass hospital.

She couldn't tear her gaze away from the picture. Why would Jared give this to her? It was hard enough for her to accept her responsibility at the lack of fairy-tale quests solved over the last two months and her brother's death in the fire. She wasn't sure what would happen to her if she lost her mom.

She was about to flip the notebook closed when a shadow fell across the page. Mina quickly covered up the drawing with her arms and looked up into the smiling face of—Brody.

"Hey, Mina, looks like we have home room together."

Please, she thought, *let that be it for the questions.* As much as she wanted to speak to Brody, to hug him, to kiss him, to tell him she had feelings for him, and to please explain the kiss at the end of last year, she couldn't. Not without falling apart like a blubbering baby.

The teacher, Mr. Ames, began going over the morning's announcements, club activities, and sports tryouts. Brody took the desk right in front of her and didn't turn back for more conversation. Nan never walked through the door, probably meaning she was in a different home room, since this year they'd organized the students by alphabet. And Taylor was at the end. Luckily for her, she had the most laid-back class of the day with Brody, but unluckily for her, she also sat in the seat farthest from the door.

When the announcements were over, they had free time since it was the first day of school and there wasn't any

Fable

homework or tests to study for. But Mr. Ames made his way over to the back of the room and straight for Mina's desk.

He knelt down to be at eye level with her and took a deep breath. "We heard about the fire and the death of your brother. The school faculty and I know that this is a difficult time for you. If you need anything, please speak up and let one of us or the school counselor know."

He had been trying to speak quietly, but it was obvious by the stiffening of Brody's shoulders and the audible intake of breath in front of her that he'd overheard their teacher. Well, that was one less awkward conversation she would have to have.

Brody turned and whispered quietly to Mr. Ames, "If the school and faculty wanted to support Mina and her family, why didn't any of you come to the funeral?"

The question had taken the teacher aback, and Mina mentally cheered on Brody.

When Mr. Ames went back to the front of the room, Brody spun around in his chair with pity in his eyes.

"That wasn't sincere. They should have been there to show support. I should have been there for you more."

Her heart felt like it was being stabbed repeatedly over and over with a knife. "Why? You're not responsible for me. You're not my boyfriend." She could tell the words hurt him a little, because his cheeks reddened and then his eyes dropped down to stare at her lips. She knew he was remembering their shared kiss

55

at the hospital. There was no denying the attraction…or the fact that an hour later he was kissing her best friend.

Mina sucked in her breath when she saw where his eyes lingered. She, too, began to remember their kiss, but she remembered a different kiss, their first kiss on the school stage, a kiss that he would never remember. Her heart began to pound, and her lungs screamed for air at the intensity that was building to a crescendo.

He reached out and touched the top of her hand, and Mina jumped in her seat, causing her notebook to fall off the desk and onto the floor. He moved his hand from hers and bent to pick up her notebook. She felt a loss as soon as he moved his hand, and he didn't put it back when he handed her the notebook.

"Well, I thought at least we were close enough—" he began.

"No, Brody…we're not. We won't ever be close, because my *best friend* means the world to me." Her emphasis on the word "friend" left him no room to argue.

The spell was definitely broken, and she needed to get her heart under control. This was no longer her boyfriend.

"Does Nan know that we…?" Brody gestured between the two of them, referring to their kiss.

"That night at the hospital? No way…not if I can help it. You're not going to tell her, either…right?" She gave him a pleading look.

Fable

"Uh, no," he said quickly. He seemed tense, like he was upset that she hadn't told Nan.

It took every ounce of Mina's willpower not to do a face plant into the table. That wasn't exactly what she was hoping for, and now she was dying for the bell to ring.

Thankfully, he turned around and began talking to one of his water polo friends. When the bell did ring, she was up and out the door first, despite being in the corner. She was surprised to see that Jared was already outside the door, waiting for her, and put his hand on the small of her back to lead her to the side of the door.

"How was it? Think you can survive five more periods?" he asked softly.

Brody walked out the door behind Mina and saw the placement of Jared's hands on her. He scowled.

A squeal could be heard down the hall, followed by the pattering of running feet. Mina was bombarded by blonde hair, strawberry perfume, and the blubbering crying form of Nan Taylor, who clamped onto her neck. Nan's long blonde hair was in a side ponytail, and she wore a teal lacy shirt and denim shorts, a zillion colored bangles on her wrists. Her cute nose and eyes were red from crying.

"I-I-I can't believe it. He can't be gone." She started to cry loud and hard, and Brody looked uncomfortable and unsure of how to comfort his girlfriend, since she was wrapped around Mina's neck.

No one understood Charlie like Nan. The two were the best of friends and had a dynamic brother-sister relationship, teasing and name-calling included, that Mina envied. Nan was an only child and treated Charlie like her own brother. Mina was feeling really guilty now for not finding a way to get hold of Nan when she was in New York at drama camp.

Mina felt her eyes start to tear up, but she held them back and comforted Nan. Students stopped and stared, and quite a few made rude comments, but Jared's and Brody's stern looks kept them at bay, giving the girls time to confer.

There were a few girls who didn't take the hint. Savannah White and Pricilla Rose—both girls stopped and rolled their eyes. Savannah used to date Brody at the beginning of last year, and now she had it out for anyone who stood between her and him. She looked killer in her designer skirt, lace tank top, and bejeweled flats. Her white-blonde hair was in its signature high ponytail, and her lips had enough gloss you could almost see your reflection in them. Pri wore a similar but toned-down version of Savannah's outfit.

"So I heard on the news that the Tard died and your house burnt down. I bet secretly you're relieved you don't have to live with him anymore in that dump."

The whole commotion in the hallway immediately stopped, as if her words had been spoken over the intercom. It became so quiet that you could hear Mina's and Nan's sharp intakes of breath. Mina wasn't prone to violence and was about to think of something mean to say back to Savannah, but she didn't have a chance to, because Nan Taylor, perky, happy-go-lucky Nan Taylor, pulled back her fist and punched Savannah in the face.

Savannah wasn't prepared, and fell to the floor. Nan stood over her shocked face and yelled, "No way was he handicapped, or different. He was the most special, coolest, and smartest kid ever. And the world is a much sadder place because he's not here. And don't you ever, EVER, insult him again!" Nan shook with anger.

The hall was full of students and teachers, and one by one they started to clap. The clapping got louder, and Nan's hands went to her mouth in shock. She looked at what she had done, and her face grew red.

She turned and threw her arms around Mina, and spoke quickly. "I'm sorry. I'm so sorry. That was wrong of me. I'm probably going to get in a lot of trouble for this, but it was worth it. No one insults our Charlie." She pulled herself away and walked toward the principal's office, her head held high. Savannah, during the commotion, started screaming and crying, and was sniveling about Nan being a "bully, brat, and jealous of her good looks."

Mr. Ames was trying to hide the smile on his face as he helped up Savannah and led her to the principal's office right behind Nan. The second bell rang, and no one was heading to the next class. They were all right where they'd stopped, talking and texting about the altercation.

It was Mrs. Colbert, with her short hair and blue wing-tipped glasses, who put her fingers to her mouth and whistled loudly, causing those nearest her to cover their ears.

"That's enough chitter chatter. Get to class, or you'll *all* have detention!" she yelled loudly.

Brody took off, heading to his next period. Jared looked a little scared at the sight of Mrs. Colbert, and ducked behind a group of students and disappeared. Mina was left alone and out of sorts, but she was able to make it to her next class. She was a zombie the entire time and was pretty sure the teacher called on her a few times, but she was useless until lunchtime. Jared met her after fourth period and walked the lunch line with her. When Mina went to grab her tray of pizza, cut carrots, and chocolate milk, Jared swiped it up and carried it out the main lunchroom and down the hall.

"Hey!" she called after him, while trying to catch up with his longer legs. He didn't stop, but turned and headed out a side door that led outside. Finding a comfortable spot under a tree, he finally placed her tray down and waited for her to sit.

She should have been upset by his actions, but after looking around outside at the lack of students, and the quiet calm shade the tree provided, she actually felt grateful. It was still incredibly hot out, but she could put up with that in exchange for solitude. Or almost solitude.

Fable

Mina took a bite of her pizza, which tasted like paper covered in cheese. She forced it down and then took to breaking her carrot sticks into miniscule pieces.

"What did those carrots ever do to you?" Jared joked.

"Charlie hated carrots, so he used to do this to them to make it look like he'd eaten them, or make them small enough to hide under the mashed potatoes."

"Smart kid."

"Yeah, he is...or was." An awkward silence rose between them, and Jared looked like he had something bothering him.

"Look, Mina, you can't let his death affect you like this. You need to move on. Prepare yourself for whatever crazy scheme the Fates will send your way."

"I know. I'm just not sure that I have the heart for it anymore."

Jared's cheek ticked in anger. "I know you lost your brother, but you can't give up so easily."

"Why do you even care?"

"I care! I thought for sure since you figured out the tie between the Grimoire and me that you would at least summon me or talk to me. But you ignored me the whole summer. I was angry with you!"

"And I was confused and hurt. I'd lost my boyfriend...again."

"Get over the human. It's obvious that you two aren't meant to be together."

"Well, maybe we could have a chance if the Fae stopped interfering with my life."

"We just saved him the trouble of dumping you after he realized how close he came to being saddled with you and your emotional baggage," Jared fumed.

"I don't have emotional baggage," Mina whispered, choking on the pain his words caused.

"Yes, you do. You've got enough emotional baggage that you could open up your own airline." He began to tick the items off his fingers. "Let's see: abandonment issues, low self-esteem, jealousy issues…and you're obsessive."

Mina was stunned and shocked at his assessment of her. Whether he was right or wrong, it didn't matter. What mattered was the fact that he was talking down to her.

"I don't have to take this from you. Maybe I was right all along to not talk to you. It's obvious you have no compassion or understanding of a human's feelings. Which are completely normal for a teenager who was unjustly saddled with a curse that's destroyed her whole family. I'm sorry if I have the emotional stability of a teeter-totter right now, but that's better than you, who has the emotional maturity of a rock."

She squeezed her carton of chocolate milk so hard that a chocolate fountain spewed out the top to run down her hand onto her jeans. Mina's eyes opened wide in shock, and she dropped the carton on Jared's lap. He jumped up faster than lightning and began to dance.

Fable

Mina looked at Jared's shocked face and her messy lap, and began to laugh and couldn't stop. She laughed so hard she snorted, and then laughed some more because of it. Jared looked at her strangely and started to chuckle as well. He knelt down with napkins and dabbed at her jeans in the most awkward way. Mina swatted his hands away and grabbed the napkins from him. It wouldn't matter; she would once again have an embarrassing chocolate milk incident to write in her notebook of Unaccomplishments and Epic Disasters—if she still had it. Maybe she needed to start a new one.

"I'm sorry," he mumbled, not looking her in the eyes.

"I'm the one who spilled milk on you. I'm the one who should be sorry." She still couldn't catch her breath.

Jared had sobered up pretty quick. "No, you know what I mean. I didn't really mean any of those things."

"Then why would you say them?"

"You were burying yourself so deep in your misery that you were becoming numb to your surroundings, which leaves you vulnerable to an attack. I was trying to break you out of it, and was aiming to make you feel a different emotion. I figured anger would have been the easiest one to get you to feel, but I completely disregarded joy. I forgot how easy it is to make you humans laugh." He stood back up; a large chocolate stain ran down his pants. His face kept shifting from utter disgust at the milk on his clothes to remorse for hurting her.

She couldn't help it—she started laughing again. Even though his reasoning behind being rude to her was terrible, the laughter did help her the rest of the day. She was even able to raise her hand in class and answer two questions. She didn't believe it, but Jared's attempt at caring by pretending not to...worked.

Sara even noticed a slight change in her when she picked her up from school.

"Did you have a good day, honey?" she asked while frowning at the brown stain on Mina's pants.

"No, it was awful. The worst first day of school ever," Mina answered with a huge grin on her face.

Eight

Nan was rightfully suspended from school for a week. Which left Mina completely defenseless against Ever's constant French-fry thieving. The pixie had a serious thing for French fries. But it also put her right between Brody and Jared.

Lunch period was painful and awkward. Whenever Brody tried to ask Mina a question, Jared would interject and turn the subject back to Nan. Ever, frustrated by Jared's lack of attention, turned to tossing food in the air and catching it in her mouth. It wasn't until Ever almost choked on one of the French fries that the boys calmed down their feud and turned to helping the girl not choke to death.

For once in her life, Mina was thankful for the pixie's interference. Now, if she could only interfere and find a way for Mina to get out of her Tuesday/Thursday P.E. class.

Mina was terrified of gym class, and tried hard to stay out of the way of the more athletic students. She also hated gym because she was forced to change into stupid gym shorts, and she always thought her legs were too skinny, like a chicken or duck. The other girls wore their gym clothes like they walked straight off the runway. Mina's gym clothes, no matter how she folded them, always looked like they came out of a hamper. She was hoping today was a running day instead of something like baseball or basketball. She actually liked running the mile on the school's track. There was less chance of her injuring herself or others.

But today was not going her way at all. It wasn't a track and field day. It was worse. They were playing flag football. It used to terrify her to have the football and have the more aggressive boys shoot right toward her, intent on ripping her flags off.

A few times last year she was bowled over in the process, and once she even ripped off her own flag and threw it on the ground in front of T.J. when he was about to tackle her. This made her a very unpopular teammate. So her goal for this year was to stay out of the way.

Mina was late because somehow her shoelaces were in incredible knots. She threw her shoes over her shoulder and ran out to the field in her socks. Once there, she plopped on the ground behind the girls and desperately tried to untangle the knots in the laces to get her shoes on. The team captains were chosen, but she didn't even notice.

Briefly she stopped and tried to get a head count to see if there would be too many players and she could sit out. Or better yet, next time she should try to get a doctor's note that read, "Mina Grime is unable to participate in any sports due to the hazard to other students' health." The teams began their draft; Mina knew her name wouldn't be called anytime soon, so she continued attacking her laces. She was wrong.

"Mina!"

It wasn't hard to miss his golden voice calling her name over the crowd of students, loud and clear, and she froze in her spot on the grass. When she didn't immediately come forward, he called her name a second time. Mina attacked her laces with a vengeance and finally stuffed her foot into the last shoe. The girls around her parted, and everyone saw her scramble up from the ground and wipe furiously at the grass clinging to the back of her shorts. She took a deep breath, carefully tucked her ponytail over her shoulder, and walked toward the voice that had called her name.

Her face turned bright red again when she walked over to Brody. He smiled widely; she frowned at him and took her place on his team. She could see the glares she was getting from half of the girls and the incredulous looks from all the boys.

What was the most popular boy in school doing, picking the slowest girl to be on his team? Once again, the whispers followed, and she could make out some mean-spirited name-calling. But she didn't care. She raised her chin proudly and swore to herself she would try hard, and not let Brody down. As long as she didn't get the ball, she would try to pretend she knew what she was doing.

The infamous flag football draft continued with the rest of the boys being picked, followed by the girls. Mina watched as Tiffany was placed on the red team, followed by Pricilla Rose on the yellow team. One by one the girls were divided. Wide-eyed with disbelief, Mina was flabbergasted that Brody purposely avoided picking Savannah White for his team. As mathematical fate would have it, she ended up on the opposing team as the last girl standing, a spot that was usually reserved for Mina.

It was an awkward moment, but not for long, as Savannah threw Mina her renowned mean-girl glare, which meant *stay out of my way*. After the kick-off, the yellow team received the ball and made it to the forty-five-yard line before losing a flag. When they lined up for the second down, Savannah placed herself opposite Mina.

She couldn't help but compare herself to the extremely fit cheerleader and knew that Savannah was out to embarrass her. This only fueled Mina's fire, and she was going to take her down and not humiliate herself in the process. Well, easy enough—as long as Brody didn't pass her the ball.

But that wasn't what the hot, sweet, sensitive guy did. He added fuel to the flame by placing the ball in Mina's hands.

"Are you crazy?" she hissed.

"Run!" He laughed and slapped her on the back.

Fable

Mina stared at the ball in her hands and looked up at Savannah's face, which turned downright ugly as she ran straight for Mina's waist and came away with two yellow flags only seconds into the play.

Mina was humiliated, and she had to go retrieve the flags from the place where Savannah snottily threw them to the ground. She reattached them and decided it was going to stop here and now. The bullying, the name-calling. She couldn't let Nan fight her school battles for her. She was a Grimm, wasn't she? She'd fought bears, dragons, Reapers, but she couldn't handle a single mean-spirited girl?

Mina gritted her teeth, dug her heels into the ground, and reached deep within herself to a hidden place that she didn't know existed. She was only just learning the capabilities that came to all Grimms when they repeatedly dipped into the Fae power.

Her feet began to tingle, as if they had fallen asleep, and her hands grew warm. She could have sworn that she could even hear better. Her breathing picked up as her muscles flexed, and a maniacal grin formed on her face. *Is this what it's like to actively touch the Fae power?*

Savannah frowned when she saw the confident look on Mina's face, and when the third play began, she was still standing there, confused, as Mina flew around her. Like the wind, she turned, twisted, and dodged around Savannah, and took off running toward the end zone and Brody. He was running, and she was keeping pace with him. Someone on the red team reached for him, and she screened him. It felt good to protect the guy she liked.

She wasn't even winded as yard by yard she stayed dead even with him and interfered again as another player came to steal his flag.

Not happening, she thought, and quickly turned around and ran backward and slowed to get in his way.

"Move it!"

"Make me!" she yelled back, grinning from ear to ear. She could hear the yell of her team as Brody crossed the end zone. No one else was even near them.

Brody ran back and high-fived her. "Nice screening. I didn't know you were that fast."

"Neither did I." She beamed, feeling glorious.

There were others who took notice of Mina's newfound confidence. The coach even tried to convince her to go out for track. Boys started to pay attention to her, not for her looks, but for her tomboyishness—which made her one of them. Brody didn't like the attention she was getting, and it was obvious. He kept moving her closer to him until she was playing running back.

It felt great the one time that Savannah had the football, and Mina got to rip both of the flags from her belt in rapid retaliation. Mina was so fast that she was snagging flags left and right. It was a close game. They were tied, and her team had the ball.

Brody counted down, and she ran. She heard Steve yell, "Mina's open—toss it to Mina!"

Wait? What? OH NO! Not quite prepared, she looked up and freaked as the spiraling pigskin was coming straight toward her head. Without thinking, she reached up and confidently caught the football. Now what? Oh, yeah, run. She took off toward the end zone, both of her yellow flags still attached to her band. Frank was running toward her arm, outstretched to end her run, but no, she wasn't going to let that happen. She pumped her legs harder and bore down the field, dodging right, then left, staying out of the reach of the other team's defenders.

She could see it! The goal, and nothing was going to stop her. She didn't know what was happening, but whatever it was, she liked it. Especially when she carried the football into the end zone and still had all of her flags. Mina did a little victory dance and tried to toss the ball on the ground in celebration, only for it to bounce up and hit her in the face. Yes, she was faster and stronger, but still as uncoordinated ever.

Her hands flew to her face and her swelling nose. She pulled her hand away and saw blood.

Brody was the closest to her. "Ouch! Are you okay? Do you need to go to the nurse?"

Mina rolled her eyes. Of course, he would see her act of stupidity.

Coach Beeber had caught up to them and echoed Brody's previous statement.

"No, I don't need the nurse, just a towel and some ice," Mina mumbled through her bloody hand.

"I'll escort her," Brody announced.

"To the girls' locker room?" Coach Beeber scoffed. "She's a big girl, Carmichael. If she can't find the ice pack and sit in the girls' locker room for a spell, then I feel bad for her. Besides, there's still ten minutes of class left."

Brody turned scarlet. Coach Beeber turned to her. "Now, if you think you need to go to the school nurse, don't hesitate for a moment.

Mina nodded her head in understanding and slowly jogged across the field to the gym's blue double doors. She slipped into Coach Beeber's office and headed to the small mini fridge. She was quite familiar with the location of the ice packs. In fact, she probably had one with her name on it. Sure enough, there was the cute bear-shaped ice pack. She grabbed it out of habit and retreated to the girls' locker room. She sat on the bench, applying pressure, and replayed the last half hour over and over in her head. When her nose finally stopped bleeding, she decided to take advantage of the empty locker room and take a shower.

She went to the last stall, turned the hot water on, and went to her locker to pull out her regular clothes, knowing the pipes needed time to heat up. With an unnatural speed, the locker roomed filled with steam, turning the ugly fluorescent white light into beautiful halos. There was something strange about the haze. The steam sparkled and glittered like gold. It was getting hard to breathe, but never before had she seen something so beautiful and unnerving at the same time.

Mina looked at the condensation building on the mirrors and carefully ran her finger across it, leaving a clean streak of her own reflection. Her finger came away covered in gold.

"What the…?"

Her hands trembled slightly as she turned on the faucet to confirm her suspicion. At first the water sputtered out clear, but then transformed before her eyes into liquid gold. Frightened, she hastily turned the faucet off. A noise clanged over in the corner of the locker room and Mina spun around, her heart pounding so unnaturally loud even to her own ears. Something by the ceiling darted out and flew to another iron beam. It was a bird.

Her hand flew to her heart in relief. This wasn't the first time a bird had found its way into the girls' locker room and scared quite a few girls. They'd had the oddest animals, birds and snakes, creep in through open locker room windows. This bird was large like an eagle, but its wings glistened, reflected as if it was made of an unnatural material, and the tips were glowing like flames.

The sound of the metal shower knob cranking, followed by the silence of the previously running shower, alerted Mina to the presence of another person in the locker room, which drew her attention from the bird. The tingling building within her warned her it was Fae.

"Hello," Mina called. "Is someone there?" No answer came forth, but she could hear the echo of boots on the cement floor. She couldn't tell from what direction it came, though. The steam had become unnaturally thick, and the gilded haze was starting to leave trails of golden dew on her skin. She looked down, and goosebumps rose up on her arms. Mina flung open the nearest locker and reached in to grab the first object she could find to defend herself. It was a baseball bat. She'd take it.

There! She saw it. A slight movement to her left. She shifted her feet and kept the locker at her back, and tested her grip on the metal bat. Something was moving toward her out of the haze. Mina had just taken aim at the shadowy figure walking toward her when something flew from above and attacked her. Pain laced through Mina's hand as the bat fell from her grip. She looked down and saw three bright red slashes along the top of her hand. The maniacal bird turned in the rafters and came back for another attack. Out of self-preservation and instinct, she dived and rolled out of the way.

She jumped to her feet without her weapon.

"Why, hello, dear, looking for this?" The haze had parted to reveal a man, smiling profusely while holding her baseball bat. He was good-looking, in his mid-thirties; his copper-colored hair was pulled into a ponytail. His pale skin did nothing but accentuate his haunting hazel eyes. Even in the heat of the sauna-like locker room, he wore a three-piece suit embellished with a cornucopia of golden trinkets, leather, and pockets that completed his odd ensemble, making him look a mixture of dashing and hodgepodge. But it was his hat that told her he was her midnight stalker. With the top hat and its gold feather, the silhouettes were identical.

"Who are you? And why are you following me?"

"Temple. My name is Temple, and I have a proposition for you." He held up his gloved hand and tipped his top hat toward her. "Hear what I have to say first, and then I promise you, if you want to scream, then do so. But I think you will be extremely interested in what I have to offer."

Mina hesitated when she saw that he held the bat and slowly took off a gloved hand and touched it, turning the aluminum bat into gold. She swallowed and then faced the stranger. So far he hadn't made an attempt to harm her, and it wouldn't hurt her to at least listen.

"Okay, what is it that you want?" she asked hesitantly.

"I want you to procure an item for me. That is all. Say you will get this item for me, and I will give you all of this," he motioned to the golden bat, "and more." He reached toward her shoulder; even his fingernails were long and golden.

Mina flinched, but he reached past her into the opened locker to withdraw a single expensive sandal that she recognized as belonging to Savannah. As soon as his hand touched the sandal, it immediately turned to gold. He smiled crookedly when he saw her eyes widen, and dropped the sandal into her hands. Mina immediately tossed the shoe back into the locker.

"The Midas touch?" she asked.

He frowned at her. "No, more like the family trait. So you see, you can be rich beyond your wildest dreams. Rich enough to impress your young human and maybe even steal him back from your best friend."

"How do you know about that? How could you possibly—"

"I make it my business to know these things. So, what do you say? Procure the item for me, and I'll make you rich."

Mina looked at the gold sandal and bat, and back at the man. Every inch of her knew better than to make a deal with the Fae, no matter what the cost.

"No, there's no amount of money in the world that would make me enter into a bargain with you." She tried to step around him, but he held out his arm, blocking her.

"Wait! Everyone has their price, and no one says no to me." He frowned at her.

"Well, I just did say no."

"That's only because you haven't heard my *other* offer." Temple took off his hat and brushed imaginary dust off it.

"It wouldn't matter, because the answer is still no. You have nothing I want," Mina said.

Fable

"Ah, and that's where I beg to differ. I do have something you want. I make sure to always have something someone wants." He placed the hat back on his head.

"Are you deaf? Because I just said no." She placed her hands on her hips and raised her chin.

"What about your brother Charlie? Such a quiet boy, but charming all the same. He misses you, I can tell."

Mina came alive with anger. "What do you mean, Charlie? He died in the fire!"

"Come now, you can't really believe that!" He touched his hat and fingered the golden feather. "I sent my servant to retrieve the boy for me and destroy your home. Now he is mine. I will trade him to you for the item I want you to procure, and nothing more. His life for my item. It's fair—what do you say?"

Mina stared at Temple in horror. "You did this? You planned this from the beginning, stealing my brother to make sure I couldn't say no! What kind of monster are you? It's been weeks. Why now? You could be lying. Why didn't you come to me that night?"

"Because you've been surrounded by Fae. What's a few weeks in the life of an eternal Fae? I'm patient. I've been waiting for hundreds of years—what's a few mere weeks? But if you fail, Charlie is mine forever."

Tears of relief started to trail down Mina's cheeks. "What is it I have to do?"

"A favor, one itsy-bitsy, teeny-weenie favor. A piece of cake for a Grimm." His smile was so sweet it was sickening.

"What is it?" Mina said, her heart dropping into her stomach, since she already had an idea.

"You have a wonderful book. The Grimoire—its power is unmatched…except for one other book. Its twin. I want that book."

"Impossible," she blurted out quickly.

Temple's expression started to get angry, but then he was able to calm himself down. "Unfortunately, I know you are wrong. My plans are always…perfect."

"How do you expect me…? How could I possibly…?" She couldn't finish; she knew nothing about the Fae world or how to cross into it. It was a hopeless quest.

But weren't all quests hopeless at one time or another? If her ancestors hundreds of years ago figured out how to cross over, then how much harder could it possibly be now, in the twenty-first century?

"I don't know how to go about it. I don't know how to cross over," Mina said.

"Ah, where's the fun in that? Besides, I'm confident you'll figure it out. I find that those with the most to lose tend to be the most motivated. So are we in agreement?"

"I have no choice," Mina mumbled. "I have to try to save Charlie."

Fable

Temple bent down and picked up a bobby pin, and motioned for her to hold her finger up in the air. She did so, and he pricked her finger, drawing blood. As her blood soaked the bobby pin's edge, it began to turn gold. He smiled and opened his jacket, revealing an array of pockets and containers with various gold objects, each with a small bloodstain on them, evidence of other bargains and transactions he'd made. She could see a pencil, a knife, a large spindle, and her heart stopped cold.

"Lest you not know what you have done. You've made a deal that cannot be undone." He patted his jacket happily.

"Who are you?" she asked in dread, knowing deep down who she'd just made a bargain with, but needing to know if she was right.

"I told you my name is Temple."

"No, what's your full name?"

"Ah, that. Well, I'm not as famous as the rest of my family, and I've sort of inherited the family gift. But I would think you know all about that, taking on the family business and all. So I think you know what I am."

She knew—his words confirmed it. Taking of a child, items of gold, bargains. "You're a Stiltskin, aren't you?"

Temple smiled widely, revealing gold molars, removed his hat, and bowed. "Templestiltskin at your service, and by the way...I would figure out a way to cross over sooner than later. Your kind aren't meant to survive on the Fae plane. Something happens to them. They change, and not for the better. So I would get crackin', because according to my watch, you're already two weeks behind. And I want the dark prince's book."

Temple laughed, and disappeared as abruptly as he'd materialized.

Mina stared at the single drop of blood still on her finger, a painful reminder of the bargain she'd just made with a Stiltskin.

In seconds, the room was back to normal, the haze gone as the double doors leading outside burst open and girls filed in, grumbling and complaining. Mina took the gold sandal on the floor, and kicked it into the locker and slammed the door while moving over to her own locker. Hurriedly she changed, not even bothering to fix her hair or get out of her shoes. Tears of relief poured out of the corners of her eyes, and she turned to rush out of the locker room, but not before she heard a loud shriek from Savannah White.

"What in the blazes happened to my Louis Vuitton sandal?"

Nine

Her mind was numb, her heart beating uncontrollably, but somehow she made it out of the locker room and stumbled in a stupor into the hallway. She let her panic rise to the surface, and she called Jared. He appeared within seconds, took one look at her face, and grasped her arms as she almost collapsed.

"He's alive!" Mina rushed out after the shock had worn off.

"Who is?"

"My brother. That man, the one who's been following me, came here to the school. He told me he kidnapped my brother, and he's alive—on the Fae plane. All I have to do is cross over to the Fae plane and trade an item for him. Jared, I have to get him back." Her hands gripped Jared's jacket, and he very carefully separated her fingers from the jacket.

"Are you sure? I mean, how can you know that he's telling the truth? And what happened to your hand?"

"Because I know. I heard a strange sound the day of the fire. I heard it again today. It's his weird golden bird." She held up the back of her hand, showing Jared the scratches. "I know it's them. They took Charlie to the Fae plane. I have to get him back. You have to help me cross over so I can save my brother."

Jared's face paled, and he whispered his brother's name. "Mina, I can't let you do that."

"No! You have to help me, help my brother." Her words rushed out and slurred together in panic.

"Whoa, back up there, Mina. You can't go to the Fae plane." He carefully helped her stand up and took two steps away from her. The distance he was physically creating between them felt as if it was miles.

"You have to," she whispered, confused by his behavior.

"No, you can't. You don't know what's over there. It's not like your plane. It's not safe," Jared replied, and began walking away down the hall.

Mina shook herself out of her reverie and chased after him, trying to keep her voice down. "So, what? Are you saying that I should just abandon Charlie?

"No…yes…I don't know. I'm saying, think things through before you try to jump into something you know nothing about. Into a country where you don't know the rules or the lay of the land. You can't go. I won't allow it." He barely turned to answer, his hands waving in finality.

She was losing him, and they both knew it. "Just help me get over there. I can save Charlie and come back."

Jared opened his mouth to answer, but the second bell rang, announcing their tardiness. "Jeez, Mina. Let him go—he's just a human. There's a million more just like him. " He turned and walked toward his next class.

Jared avoided her for two days, refusing to come when she used the Grimoire. She had tried begging, calling, and even faked being attacked by a Fae wolf, but nothing. Jared didn't budge or show his face. Finally, on the third day, he reappeared at their cafeteria table, purposely trying to make lunch conversation awkward. Mina kept staring at Jared, who pretended to be extremely interested in his spaghetti, spinning the noodles on his fork at least a hundred times before taking a bite. She couldn't help herself—she was a bundle of excited energy and couldn't help but fumble with her straw, drop her fork on the floor twice, and even accidentally step on Brody's foot under the table. Ever giggled at Mina's obvious lack of grace and kept elbowing Jared to watch her, but he refused to budge or look.

Mina sighed and watched the clock, waiting for school to be over so she could go back to cornering Jared into helping her.

Maybe she could blackmail him? Hmm, the idea had merit. Maybe even Ever would help her do it?

Nan Taylor's voice cut through their table's quiet melancholy. "Okay, someone's gonna have to scoot, 'cause you're both in my seat."

Mina jumped up from the table, her chair making a loud screech as she hugged her friend and almost knocked over Nan's tray. Brody stood up, too, and moved down so his girlfriend could sit between him and Mina.

"You're back!"

Nan turned to face Mina and completely ignored Brody. "Yeah, I'm so glad to be back and not grounded. But I don't regret it for one minute. I have to tell you that my mom was furious and wanted to write a letter to the school, but I told her that the time fits the crime and to let it drop. Savannah might have started the fight verbally, but I took it physically where it didn't need to go. My mom still grumbles about writing a letter to the school board, though."

Nan sat down between Brody and Mina, and began to move the food items around on her plate. "I was completely bored out of my mind at home this whole week. I can't tell you all the things I concocted to keep myself busy. I had a *Glee* marathon, a Hello Kitty party for one, and I even attempted a *Project Runway* dress out of the things in our kitchen." Nan switched to a Tim Gunn impression. "I looked fabulous...and believe it or not, I made it work."

Fable

Mina started laughing...hard. Even Brody and Ever were chuckling. Jared continued to swirl his spaghetti.

Nan looked great in her jean skirt, white leggings, blue tank top, and sparkly pink nail polish, right down to her expertly fishtailed braid. Mina couldn't help but feel slightly disheveled in her discount jeans and cute rainbow tank top, blue hoodie, and Converse shoes. At least today she'd attempted to wear blush and a light pink lip gloss. She never used to compare her appearance to Nan, but now that Brody was so near both of them again, she couldn't help but let the comparisons ride out. She was definitely the ugly duckling.

"Mina," Nan interrupted her thoughts, "you look so cute today. Tell me, is it because of a guy? It is, isn't it? Who is it?"

Brody's head snapped in Mina's direction; he was obviously interested in hearing her answer, but he carefully pretended indifference as he took a swig of cola.

"NO, there's no guy. There's no one."

"Well, there should be a guy. There should be a hundred boys lined up to date my best friend. Right, Brody?" Nan cornered him with a look.

Brody almost choked on his drink, and after wiping his mouth on his jacket, he gave Nan a sheepish look. "Um, yeah, hundreds." He swallowed and stared directly into Mina's eyes.

"Well, you should set her up on a date with one of your friends, then," Nan said.

"NO!" Mina and Brody cried out in unison, while Ever pumped her fist and yelled, "YES!"

Nan started laughing, and picked up her water bottle and twisted the lid. "It's official, Bro. Tonight...double date."

"Make that a triple," Ever interrupted, looking at Jared across the table hopefully.

Jared's head snapped up, and he stared at the four of them in horror...once he realized what they were saying.

Brody groaned. Mina turned beet red, Nan laughed, and Ever glared at Jared, who finally quit playing with his food and buried his head in his hands.

Ten

"Mina, I don't think I can go through with this," Nan cried out, pacing back and forth in Mina's bedroom, her long skirt swishing back and forth, her gold-toned sandals flopping on the hardwood floor.

"Go through with what—the date?" Mina asked. She looked at herself in the mirror and sighed. This was the best she was going to look. She had pulled her long wavy brown hair into a side ponytail and let it trail down her left shoulder. She wore shorts, a sapphire-blue tank top, sandals, and a short tan jacket with an inside pocket, into which she'd tucked the smallest version of the Grimoire. She was no Nan or Savannah; she could never compete with them. But she thought she looked pretty good.

"I'm scared to go on a date with Brody," Nan admitted before crashing onto Mina's bed and staring around the room as if she was seeing it for the first time. Well, she was, but opulence or poverty never mattered to Nan. Even when Mina lived in a run- down flat above a Chinese restaurant, Nan never cared.

"But you two have been dating for four months. How could you be nervous?" Mina answered.

"It's not like you think. Our dates have consisted of mostly sitting at the lunch table the last few weeks of the school year, and a few movies. Then we went our separate ways the whole summer, and we barely talked, Mina. This whole thing moved really fast. I'm not really sure what to think of it."

"Why didn't you talk to him about it?"

"I don't know. I mean, he woke me out of a coma with a kiss, so that means he must like me. And of course it was all really sweet the way Brody looked after me when I got out of the hospital. He pulled the chair out for me, carried my books. But we've only ever kissed one time after that, and I was the one who instigated it—and that was before we left for the summer. It's been really awkward since. It's like we're better friends than boyfriend and girlfriend. We used to call each other every day, then it became every other day, and now once a week. I mean, it's Friday night! Our first Friday night back together for the whole summer, so of course it means a date. But please, oh, please, Mina. I can't go on this date alone. What if my fears are correct—what if we're only friends?"

Nan's words made Mina's spirit soar and then come crashing down in a mash-up of confusion and hurt for her friend's plight. It was what she secretly wanted to hear, but at the same time, she would never wish for this to happen to her best friend. Oh, the mixed feelings it created, and right in the middle of her own nightmarish plot of trying to save her brother. She was so torn, but she needed to get Jared on her good side and help her cross over.

"It will be fine," Mina said, encouraging her. "If you need a quick escape, I'll just dump my pop on myself, and we'll have to go home early. How's that?"

Nan's blue eyes widened in disbelief. "You would do that for me?"

"Well, it's a fifty-fifty shot it's going to happen anyway tonight, so yeah, I would do that for you."

"Mina, you are the best friend ever!" Nan hugged Mina before they headed downstairs to wait for the rest of their troupe.

Sara was sitting quietly in a rocking chair in the library, staring at a blank spot on the wall where a very obvious picture had previously hung. Mina knew from the size of the spot that it was where her father's picture had been. Did Sara somehow know?

As Nan chatted and led the way to the foyer, Mina couldn't help but slow down to stare at her mom. Was there a difference in her? For once she wasn't sad; she was rocking in a chair, humming to herself. Her mom was behaving strangely, and not just since Charlie had disappeared, but over the last few months. She wasn't jumping at every noise, threatening to pick up and move across the country. She was becoming normal. The hairs on the backs of Mina's arms rose in trepidation. What was happening to her mom? There was nothing obviously wrong, but nothing obviously right, either.

"Mom," Mina called, walking softly to stand by her chair. Sara was wearing an oversized gray knit sweater wrapped around her. Her brown hair had started to fall out of its bun. Something sparkled around her wrist, and Mina saw a simple charm bracelet, probably some gift they had given their mom years before and didn't remember.

Sara's rocking stopped, and with it her humming. "Yes, dear?"

"I'm leaving to go out with my friends. Are you going to be okay?"

Sara began rocking again. "Oh, yes, I'm thinking of all the rooms in this house that need to be cleaned. I think I'm going to start with that storage room you found."

"No, not that one! It's just junk in there. Why don't you take the closets on the other side of the house? When I have time, I'll work in there."

"That would be nice. What a sweet daughter I have," she intoned, and stared at the wall. "I wish I could have had more kids like you."

Mina stepped away from her mom, tears starting to build in her eyes.

Fable

"Mom, you did. Don't you remember Charlie?" Mina had been unable to tell her mother about the deal she'd made with Temple, for fear of getting another of the accusing looks Sara had bestowed upon Mina after the fire. It was obvious that Sara, even though she didn't mean to, still blamed her daughter. What would happen if Mina were unable to save Charlie? What would her mom think of her then?

Sara stopped rocking once more. "Charlie? That's a nice name. If I ever have a boy, I'll think I'll name him Charlie."

"Mom, you do have a son named Charlie. Charlie's nine years old now. Remember?"

"Hmm." Sara closed her eyes and drifted off to sleep.

Nan grabbed Mina's arm and pulled her out of the room. "Mina, give her time. It will be okay."

"Are you sure?"

"Not really, but she's been through a lot, and she could be having a memory lapse. I'd say check on her when we get home, and if you want, I can have Robert come over and take a look at your mom."

Mina had momentarily forgotten that Nan's mom had gotten married over the summer to Dr. Robert Martin. That was all the reassurance she needed. She didn't know what she would do if Sara went to the hospital and she was left in the house all alone.

"I guess a few hours will be fine. I would hate to take her to the hospital if it's just a short spell." The words hung in the air, and Mina's mind began to whirl with possibilities. She didn't have time to continue the thought further, because the silver box buzzed.

She ran to the box and hit the green button. "Hello?"

Static, and then she could hear two voices arguing in the background. "Why in the world are we pushing the button?" She recognized Ever's voice.

"Because that's the way *they* do it," Jared's voice argued back.

"Well, we are not like *them*. You're a prince. Just wave your hand and—"

Mina quickly pushed the "open" button for the driveway gate, hoping to cut off Ever and Jared's Fae magic conversation before Nan overheard.

A few seconds later, Jared pulled up in an orange 1969 Ford Boss 429 Mustang, which she knew was really Fae magic at work. Another car came up the driveway, and Mina was surprised to see Brody's new car he'd gotten after the accident, a black Escalade. The driver's window rolled down, and Brody leaned his head out the window. "You ladies ready?"

Nan smiled widely but gripped Mina's hand nervously. "You bet."

Mina tried to crane her neck to see who was in the car with Brody, but she couldn't see who the passenger was. A second later, the other door opened, and someone stepped out. He was tall and broad-shouldered, with copper-colored hair and warm hazel eyes. He wore jeans, a white polo shirt, and a jacket. Mina scanned her memory of her high school yearbook and couldn't place him anywhere. He was cute, that was for sure, and her heart did a small nervous flutter of anticipation. Now it was Mina's turn to grip Nan's hand really hard.

Brody hopped out of the driver's seat, walked over to Nan, and put an arm around her shoulders. "Hey, Mina, this is Reid Stone."

"Nice to meet you, Mina," Reid announced.

Her head snapped up, and she responded softly, "Nice to meet you, too. You don't go to Kennedy, do you?"

"No, I actually know Brody through a mutual friend of ours."

"Oh," she said sadly, wondering if Brody had been unable to find anyone from their own school who would actually go on a date with her.

"Wow, Brody. You forgot to tell me that she was so cute." Reid punched his friend in the shoulder.

Brody frowned, and he was visibly grinding his teeth. "Didn't I?"

Jared never got out of the car, and revved the engine irritably in response to their chitchat. "Let's get this over with. Unless you want to hit the nine o'clock showing of *Death Pledge*, we need to get going."

Mina hurried over. Reid opened the rear door for her and she slid into the car, her skin slightly catching on the leather seats. Reid slid in after her and turned so he could face her in the seat.

"So, Mina, tell me about yourself."

She felt uncomfortable, nervous, and she felt like she was going to be sick. She watched Nan jump into the front seat with Brody, and she looked just as nervous, even more so. Maybe the two of them were not meant to date…ever. Neither one of them had any luck so far keeping the guys they really wanted.

"Um, let's see. I'm a junior at Kennedy High, and I like…" She blanked. Completely blanked. In that second she realized how utterly boring and plain she was. Anything even remotely interesting wasn't something that she could come right out and say. *I chase down fairy-tale villains in my spare time and entrap them in my magic book.* Yeah, she couldn't say that. "…I like my family and kids and animals."

Nan turned around and made a disgusted noise at her. "You sound like you're being interviewed for Miss America. Here, let me help. She's artistic, one of the best in her advanced art class. Her pencil sketches, if you can ever get her to show them to you, are phenomenal, along with her pastels. She likes to read, but not that smutty stuff—classics, and books that have depth to them. She remembers everything someone tells her and has a knack for finding the good in everyone."

Brody looked back at her through the rearview mirror. "And she kills at flag football. Don't let her fool you. She's got some fight in her."

Fable

Mina blushed, and Reid laughed. "I'll remember that."

Because Nan was a great icebreaker, the drive to the movie theater went by fast. She learned that Reid was the youngest of five brothers. His family was all lawyers, of a sort, and that he was lined up to work in the family business when he was done with school. He liked working with metals, welding and sculpting.

She felt herself smiling and laughing at Reid. When they arrived at AMC Theaters, she was prepared to buy her own ticket, but Reid wouldn't let her. He bought both of their tickets, two drinks, and a large popcorn. She was secretly relieved that this date was actually going well.

Jared grudgingly paid for Ever's ticket and her box of Sour Patch Kids. Ever flipped out and began to dance around in excitement when she saw that the theater also sold packages of Pixie Stix.

Nan ran ahead to the theater, then came back and announced that the theater was packed and that they would have to split up. Mina bit the inside of her cheek to keep from making a terrified face, but they all filed into the darkened room and tried to find seats that weren't so close they would have neck aches from looking straight up.

Brody and Nan found seats a few rows in front of them and to their left. Jared and Ever ended up in the very back row. Mina and Reid found seats on the right side of the theater, next to an overly large man with a beard and glasses who had enough popcorn and snacks to last for three movies. Most of the teens had their phones out and were texting or tweeting while they waited for the movie to start. Reid leaned back and stretched out his long legs in front of him, and stared at her thoughtfully.

"So I see you're not that fond of texting," Mina said, after noticing that he hadn't pulled out a cell phone, either.

"Nah, don't see what the big deal is about those things."

It was an odd choice of words, and Mina meant to ask him about it when the lights dimmed and the previews started, which ninety percent of them turned out to be commercials for Toyotas, Coca-Cola, and "please turn off your cell phone" warnings.

The movie finally began, and Mina had to squint when the 3D effects started. The red and blue lines made her dizzy, so she reached over and held out her hand to Reid expectantly.

He looked at the screen, completely baffled, and his face was scrunched up in disgust.

"Uh, the glasses," Mina teased him.

"What?" He looked irritated.

"The 3D glasses they gave you when you bought the tickets."

"Oh, those." He reached into his jacket pocket and pulled out two pairs of plastic glasses and handed one of them to Mina. He watched her put them on and mimicked her. "Ah, that's better." He smiled and settled in to watch the movie.

Fable

He sure was an odd one, she thought to herself, but quickly forgot as the first action scene filled the screen. A girl was running and being chased by a man through dark back alleys. The scene was very similar to her own life and made her feel slightly uncomfortable. Reid leaned forward and jumped when the action scene intensified. He seemed unprepared for the 3D effects. She reached forward to take a handful of popcorn, and he reluctantly moved the bucket closer to her.

Gee, maybe she'd spoken too soon about a good date. It seemed like as soon as they split from the group, he dropped the façade. He was acting as if he was more interested in the movie than her. She should have expected that, and been prepared. If she were smart, she would have slipped a book in with her, which she had done in the past, and turned around in her seat and read by the light of the movie screen when the movie was something dumb.

Her eyes kept drifting to watch Brody and Nan. They weren't holding hands, and neither one of them were leaning into each other. Oh, wait. Nan just jumped, and Brody put his arm around her shoulders. She watched as Nan leaned in and whispered something in his ear. Brody whispered something back, and when he turned he caught Mina's stare. His smile faltered, and Mina felt the need to do something daring. She leaned in and snuggled into Reid's shoulder. Reid looked surprised, but then he raised his arm and put it around her. Brody frowned and turned around.

After a while, she forgot about Reid, Brody, and even Jared as she became engrossed in the story unfolding before her. It was intense, about an orphaned young girl whose brother was kidnapped and held hostage. If she didn't assassinate the President, then they would kill her brother.

Mina reached her hand into the almost empty popcorn tub and realized it was starting to taste odd—like pennies. She watched as Reid's hand reached in and pulled out a few handfuls, and ate them without noticing the taste. She pulled the bucket out of his hands and looked into it. The popcorn had turned brown. He reached in for another handful, but she slapped his hand away.

"Don't eat it. There's something wrong with it." She pulled out a piece and noticed that it had flecks of color swirling around the white. She crumbled the popcorn in her fingers, and it was filled with something hard. Like wire.

"There's nothing wrong with it. It's just how I like it." Reid grabbed the bucket back from her and began eating it with a vengeance.

Mina stared at Reid. Really looked at him for the first time since she'd put on the 3D glasses. He looked different through the red and blue filter. The glasses made his copper hair seem to crackle in the light. His eyes even had a reflective glow in them. Then she saw his fingernails, and her heart caught in her throat. They were copper-colored. Not painted with nail polish, but really copper-colored. She'd seen only one other person with colored nails before...and he hadn't been there to help her.

She whipped off the glasses, and he was back to looking very human again. It was another Fae glamour. A trick. The Fae had learned long ago to hide their true natures from the physical plane. Just to be sure, Mina put the glasses back on, and once again she could see Reid's true form.

He turned his fiery eyes on her and smiled while he popped another copper-laced popcorn kernel in his mouth. She could hear the sound of metal crunching between his teeth.

"Ah, I see you've finally taken notice of me. Tonight is about to get so much more interesting."

He reached toward Mina, and his hand crackled with electricity. A loud popping sound was heard as the movie film stopped reeling. The lights went out. As the theater plunged into total darkness, the screaming began.

Eleven

The popcorn bucket flew in the air as Mina stumbled backward onto the person sitting next to her and half flipped, half slid over the row into an empty seat in front of her. It was ultimate chaos. He had somehow killed the electricity. She was sure of it. But her main worry was getting as far away from him as she could.

People were screaming and heading toward the emergency exits, the way lit by safety lights on the floor, but even those began to flicker and die out. She crawled along the filthy floor and was able to slide under the bar for the handicapped seating.

A panicked moviegoer stepped on her hand, kicked her in the stomach, but she was afraid to show herself. She needed everyone to get out of the theater, and fast. This was not the place for a fight between a Grimm and a...what?

Someone yelled her name, and she carefully peeked between the seats. She could see Nan by the emergency exits, refusing to leave the building, even though Brody was pulling on her arm. Nan screamed her name again, but thankfully Brody got her out the door to the left of the screen. People were still fighting to get out and trampling each other, but Reid was waiting for the same thing.

Mina looked back up a few rows and saw Reid standing exactly where she'd left him, smiling crazily. His hands let off a few more sparks, and he reached out to touch the person closest to him, the large bearded man still sitting and eating his extra-large tub of popcorn, undisturbed by the commotion around him. But once Reid's hand touched him, he froze and turned to stone. No, not stone, metal. His sparks lit up the theater like a strobe light.

Her heart stopped beating. "Jared," she whispered. He heard, he answered. He came out of nowhere like an avenging angel, springing on Reid's back, and they both crashed into the row in front of them, breaking chairs in the process.

Mina pulled out the Grimoire, knowing that she needed help but also needed to keep her distance at the same time. The book glowed, and it elongated into a crossbow.

Holy buckets! Mina thought. She'd better get it right on the first shot. She popped up, steadied the crossbow on the back of a seat, and took aim, but a body was being thrown at her— Jared's. She barely had time to turn before he landed on her full force and she became pinned between the seats.

"Jared!" Mina yelled at him. "Get up. Move."

He didn't answer—he couldn't. He was unconscious. All she was able to do was solicit a small groan from him as she struggled to free herself. In the commotion, she'd lost the crossbow, and it had skidded under a seat.

More flickering lights, laughter, and screaming mingled in the air. Her cheek rubbed against something sticky, but she gritted her teeth and stretched out her arm as far as she could. She could just barely reach the butt of the crossbow.

She could see him, Reid slowly stepping down, row by row. He was almost to her, and she was still wedged underneath Jared's prone form.

"Come on," she grunted, but it was too late. He was there.

He jumped the last row and stepped on her hand to keep her from touching the weapon. His confident smile faltered into a frown. "This was too easy. Too easy to manipulate the human. Too easy to make myself one of you. I was expecting more from the newest Grimm and her protector. I'm greatly disappointed. Oh, well, maybe your friend—Nan, right? Maybe she's got some fight in her."

"Hey, scumbag!" a voice yelled from behind him.

Reid looked up and received a kick in the face from Ever's big black army boot, catching him by surprise.

"You want a fight, you got it!" she cried out in full Fae glory, wings and all, as she flew just beyond his reach. Ever looked furious, Ever looked glorious. She was gone in a second, hidden in the dark theater. The emergency lights finally went

Fable

out, and Reid was forced to use whatever magic he had to create crackles of light to illuminate the theater to try to find her. But light wasn't his strength, Mina discovered. It was turning things to copper, and copper conducted electricity.

Mina struggled again, and was able to flip Jared onto his side and slide out from under him, but her weapon was now two rows down. She crawled low on her knees and tried to make it down the stairs without being seen. Ever was doing her best against the Fae, but without the element of surprise, she was obviously outmatched.

He lunged toward her and caught ahold of her boot. She screamed as it slowly turned to metal. Her wings beat wildly as she tried to pull out of his reach, but he laughed and held on, reaching with his other hand to grasp her leg.

She was out of time. Mina stood up and ran for the crossbow, cocked the string, and loaded the bolt. Without thinking she yelled out his name.

"Hey, Reid, over here." She released the arrow and prayed. With the luck of Fae magic, its aim was true, and it pierced Reid in the chest.

"Thanks for the great date. Don't call me—I'll call you," Mina chanted.

He gasped in pain and let go of Ever's leg. Her momentum made her crash into the wall, and she slid to the ground. Reid grasped the arrow protruding out of his chest. He started to laugh. "Now, there's the fight I wanted. It makes for better storytelling." More sparks danced from his fingertips, and the arrow slowly turned to copper.

"How about this for your ending?" Mina asked, holding the crossbow. She tossed the crossbow into the air toward him, and it began to glow and radiate light and slowly turn back into a book. His face froze in horror, and he tried to pull the arrow from his chest. The copper on the bolt stopped spreading and began to recede in the face of the Grimoire's power. The arrow of light became brighter and began to pull him toward the pages, like a fish on a hook.

He whimpered and turned to grasp onto something, anything. He dug his hands into the chair, but it began to give in to the powerful vortex created within the pages. Reid's body floated in the air and was slowly getting pulled into it. He worked himself hand over hand until he was holding onto the metal head of the large man he had turned to copper, but he was no match for the Grimoire.

With a final scream of defeat, Reid lost his grip and was sucked into the Grimoire. The book continued to pull, drawing popcorn buckets, drinks, candy boxes, and even a few lost cell phones into its pages. The book closed with a snap, and the theater was once again clothed in darkness. Mina could feel a suffocating sensation of power fill the room. It felt heavy, like a pressure on her chest, and she knew that in the darkness something magical was happening.

Fable

A few intense seconds went by before the power in the building came back on, and with it the overhead lights. Her hand went to protect her eyes from the extreme change from darkness to light. The theater was still destroyed. Ever was hopping toward her with one boot missing. She knelt by Jared and helped him up. He had a huge bruise on his cheek but seemed to be fine otherwise. Mina went to help Ever, and they both half carried, half dragged Jared out to the emergency exit.

A loud slurping noise echoed from behind them, and Mina snapped her head around to look at the only other inhabitant of the destroyed theater. It was the very large bearded moviegoer, fully human again, happily slurping away at his drink.

"Best 3D movie *ever*," he said.

Twelve

"What happened in there?" Nan cried out, and wrapped her arms around Mina. "It went dark. I heard a loud popping noise like gunfire. Are you okay? Is Jared okay?"

"Yeah, we're okay, but we could use help with Jared."

Brody jumped in and gripped his strong arms around Jared, and swiftly moved him away from the theater and farther into the parking lot. Groups of people stood in clusters, watching the building, pointing and snapping pictures on their phones. The fire department arrived, and more uniforms rushed into the building.

Mina collapsed on the ground next to Jared and ran her hands over his face in concern. The bruise on his cheek was getting larger, and his eyes started to flutter open.

"Hey, you," she whispered when his eyes locked onto hers. And what beautiful eyes they were. They were filled with confusion and pain, and then when he looked at her, they crinkled up just ever so slightly in a smile. In the dark parking lot his gray eyes looked almost blue, and she felt herself catch her breath. A warm hand cupped her elbow as Jared gently rubbed it in return. "Glad you're not dead." She smiled warmly.

"Takes more than a backhanded punch from a—"

"—jealous boy," Mina interrupted him, giving a quick glance at their captive audience.

His eyes widened in understanding, and he lowered his voice so she had to lean forward to hear the next words out of his mouth. "Did you get him?"

Mina looked at Ever and grinned. "Yeah, *we* got him."

Brody was shuffling back and forth uncomfortably in the cold, watching them, when he noticed their numbers. "Hey, where did Reid go?"

Mina sat back on her heels and gave Brody a disgusted look. "He left."

"What do you mean, he left?"

"Just what I said. When he didn't get what he wanted, he up and disappeared." She tried to say it with a straight face, but Ever snorted loudly from behind her.

Nan was shocked. "What a jerk! Mina, you must feel awful. He didn't try to take advantage of you, did he? I'm so mad—I want to go searching for him and give him a piece of my mind, and a kick in the rear. And Brody, why did you bring such a loser for Mina to date?"

Brody stepped back in surprise and rubbed the back of his head. "I...uh...I don't really remember why?" And it was a very good possibility that he didn't even remember meeting up with Reid, or that the Fae used persuasion to get him to do what he wanted.

A uniformed police officer came forward and began to take the statements from the crowd. The air became thick again with power, and she looked around in alarm. Jared gripped her elbow and sat up, sensing the same thing she did. Magic, but whose? Mina eavesdropped on the conversation and was surprised how quickly the stories of what had happened changed and morphed as the people were telling them. The Story was at work, covering up the incident in the theater by blanketing all of the witnesses with different versions.

It was fascinating and scary how easily the Story could manipulate people. A man wearing a plaid shirt and blue knit hat told the police he saw a guy shoot bolts of lightning from his hands, but then his eyes got heavy and his voice started to slur under the powerful persuasion of the Story. The police officer asked him to repeat what he saw, and he changed his story.

"It was fireworks. Some dude sneaked fireworks into the theater."

"No, it wasn't!" a short red-haired woman interjected. "I saw it—he had those popping firework things."

"Are you dumb? It was a government conspiracy. A soldier came in with experimental strobe lights, and he was trying to

108

hypnotize us. He was going to make us his slaves," a man in a white tank top and NASCAR hat said.

"It wasn't a guy—it was a girl, and she was flying." It was the large man from earlier, still slurping on his drink. "And I was turned to copper, but I'm all better now!"

"Are you on drugs? There was no girl, it was a group of boys, and they were lighting things on fire. I saw it and jumped up and pulled the fire alarm."

"No, I saw someone in the projector room. They let off a smoke bomb," an irritated teenager interrupted.

"I think it was a breaker. An employee messed with the circuit breakers," someone else yelled out.

Slowly the truth was covered up by so many lies that no one could determine what had actually happened. Finally, the policeman shook his head and walked away, no closer to the truth.

Jared stood up and let out a deep breath. Relieved.

"I take it you're used to this?" she asked.

"Yeah, but you never know whether or not it will clean up after itself."

"You mean your brother," she asked.

He nodded. "Can I see the Grimoire real quick?" She handed him the book, and he flipped to the end and took a look at the pencil sketch of the fight between Ever, Reid, and Mina, and whistled in surprise. "Looks like you two make quite the team."

Ever raised her chin and stepped between them. "Only 'cause I had to. You were out of the picture, so someone had to help your charge. It's not a job that I would cherish in the future. So don't get used to it."

Brody came up behind them, with an arm protectively wrapped around Nan. "Hey, the police are saying it was just some prank, and no harm, no foul, so we can all go home. The theater is giving us all free tickets to see another movie, once they open up again."

Nan was blushing profusely at the attention from Brody, and Mina couldn't help but feel sad and happy for her. The sudden onslaught of danger had thrown Brody into knight in shining armor mode again, and he instinctively reacted and protected his girl. Mina was delighted that he had protected Nan when she was unable to. How could she begrudge them happiness, if that was what they really wanted? Brody would always protect those closest to him—that was his nature. And if Nan was friends with a Grimm, than she would always need protecting, and she couldn't think of anyone more suited than Brody. Now if only she could convince her heart of it.

The ride home was silent. The gravity of what had happened in the theater caused the air to be filled with nervousness. She didn't even ask Nan and Brody what they remembered from tonight, preferring to not know how much of their minds had been tampered with by the Fae. She curled up

Fable

on the back seat and held the Grimoire close to her chest, and stared out the window into the night.

Twice she caught Brody staring at her in the rearview mirror, but she quickly looked away and pretended not to notice. The small notebook grew warm in her hands, and she flipped it open to a blank page and stared in wonder as words began to fill up its pages.

Did you enjoy your date tonight? ~T

The words appeared for a few seconds and then faded into the paper. Teague must be writing in the book on the Fae plane to make it appear in hers on the physical plane. An image appeared in her mind of the dark-haired prince leaning over a golden column in a round room. On the column sat a very large and ancient book. He was looking around to see if anyone was spying on him, and then leaned forward to write in its pages with a white quill.

She scrambled in her purse for a pen and tentatively wrote back on the Grimoire, her heart pounding with adrenaline.

He was a disappointment. I had higher expectations. But I guess I'm hard to please. She couldn't believe she was doing this, taunting the Story through the Grimoire. She didn't even know it was possible.

I'll try harder to meet your expectations next time. And you can be sure there will be a next time…and a next…and a next.

I will defeat you!

There was a long pause, and she thought that he had left and stopped writing. She stared at the page, willing an answer to appear, but nothing came. Finally, when she was about to close the book in frustration, his answer came, written slowly and deliberately.

Then I will look forward to that day when you confront me face to face.

That day may be sooner than you think, Teague.

I wouldn't expect you to be the one speaking tall tales.

Why did it seem like he was flirting with her? She could have sworn he was smiling when he wrote that, but how would she know? How could she so easily visualize him writing in the book, when she couldn't see him? Or was it because he was connected to the tales as much as she was that they were connected also. Her stomach rolled in displeasure.

Mina.

She didn't want to play this game anymore and almost stopped writing completely.

What? she finally answered.

I'm sorry.

For what?

For what I'm about to do…but then again…maybe not.

The car had pulled to a stop in front of Nan's apartment building, and Mina didn't even know how long they had been sitting there. She looked up in alarm and saw Brody lean forward and kiss Nan on the lips. It was aggressive and very unlike him, and she knew then what Teague was doing. He was pushing Brody into kissing Nan. She knew then that he was truly evil and sadistic. She slammed the notebook closed and sat on it in frustration. The slamming noise and movement from the back seat broke the spell that Brody and Nan were under. Nan flushed pink, and Brody pulled back so fast from the kiss he hit his head on the rearview mirror.

"Ouch!"

Nan wiped at her mouth with the back of her hand. Brody rubbed the back of his head and refused to look at either one of the girls. "Mina, I'm so sorry—you were so quiet I completely forgot you were back there."

"It's okay. I can call my mom to come get me, if you guys want to continue your date." Her voice sounded hollow even to her.

"No, I'll drive you home," Brody replied gruffly.

Nan smiled at him in gratitude and waved at her before she stepped out of the car and headed to the doorman. She turned right before she entered the double doors, and waved sweetly and blew a kiss toward the car. Mina had no doubt that the kiss was meant for Brody.

She stayed in the back seat of the car as Brody pulled away from the curb. The silence became deafening between the two of them. She told herself she didn't care, that Nan and Brody belonged together. But when Teague kept interfering with her friends with the sole intention of hurting her, she hated him, hated them. Being burned from a relationship was painful, and Teague had found a wound he could keep picking at to hurt her. She had almost believed him for a second when he said he was sorry. But she knew he wasn't.

After a few blocks, Brody slowed the car down and came to a stop down a road lined with darkened houses. "Would you like to sit in the front seat?"

"No, I think I'm good back here," she said stiffly.

"I really don't know what came over me," Brody said quietly, looking at her through the rearview mirror.

"She's your girlfriend—you don't need to explain yourself to me."

"No, it was inconsiderate of me, considering our past history. I'm not even sure why I drove Nan home first. It was never my intention to hurt you like that."

"I know. It's not your fault." Her heart was being twisted in a vise, and she didn't think she could handle it anymore. Quickly, she flipped open the Grimoire and pulled out her pen and tried something.

Jared, she wrote.

Mina? Wow, how are you doing this? I can see your words in my head.

Never mind that. Can you come get me…NOW?

Are you in danger?

She thought for a moment.

Yes, no. Just come get me…please.

Fable

On my way, he answered.

Brody squeezed his hands on the steering wheel and turned around in his seat to look at her. "You don't really mean that. You can't just up and forgive me for the way I've treated you. Mina, I've never been so confused before. I feel like I'm in a tug of war of emotions. When I'm with Nan, it's like a powerful force of nature and I can't fight it. I don't know how to fight it. But I feel so much for you. I don't…I'm not sure—"

Mina didn't let him finish because she saw the dual headlights coming down the road, and they slowed to a halt in front of the car. She grabbed her purse and notebook, and opened the door. Brody was surprised by her sudden exit and opened the driver's door to jump out after her.

She couldn't just abandon him without an explanation. She turned back and took a deep breath, being careful to keep her tears at bay. She stepped up to the door and closed it. Brody's warm hand came down on top of hers through the open window.

"Sometimes love is worth fighting for. And if you don't fight for it, then it slips through your fingers." She pulled her hand away.

He looked devastated, but she didn't turn back, and instead continued to walk toward the Ford Boss. Jared was being careful to not make eye contact with Brody. For once he was being the gentleman. She only hoped that she hadn't interrupted his date with Ever.

She slid into the front seat and opened the window as Brody pulled away. The rush of wind in her hair and the hum of the engine lulled her into a place of nothingness. Refusing to think of Brody, of Jared, of Teague, she concentrated on a happy place. Of a time when she was still with her brother, playing board games. Moments later Jared pulled up to the Grimm house and waited by the gate. Mina leaned forward across him and punched in the code, and the gate opened up. He drove slowly up to the front door and turned off the engine. She sat in the car, still numb, and he walked around to the passenger side.

He didn't speak, didn't ask any awkward questions, and she respected him for it. He saw that she was hurting, and he reached out to grab her arm and gave it a reassuring squeeze. She lost it. She threw herself into his arms and started crying, using him as a shoulder to cry on. He held his hands up in the air awkwardly before he wrapped them around her and let her cry herself out.

When she was done blubbering, she pulled herself away and used the sleeve of her jacket to wipe away the tears. "I'm so sorry." She sighed.

"Nonsense. I've watched many Grimms grieve over the years, and I think I like the way you do it the best," he answered.

She smiled and nodded pathetically. "It's not fair to you and Ever that I ruined your night, too."

"Hey, I may be old, but the night's young." He tilted his head, and the moonlight illuminated his swollen and bruised cheek. He noticed where she was staring and shook his head. "He sucker-punched me with a fist made of iron."

"Copper," she corrected.

"Is that so?"

"Yeah, I think he was a Stiltskin, too. How many of them are there?"

"More than you probably want to know."

"Then help me get to the Fae plane and rescue my brother." It was probably the wrong time to bring it up, but she was done wasting time. Tonight proved it. And she wasn't going to mention what she needed to do once she was over there. If Jared learned of her plan to steal the Fae book, he would definitely refuse to help her.

"Are you daft and dumb? No way." He grabbed Mina's arm, threatening her. "I won't let you throw your life away on something that is impossible."

"Every quest I attempt is a life-or-death situation. So why is it that when I want to do something it's dumb, but if it's a fairy-tale quest or creature it's different. It's because finding Charlie doesn't help break the curse, isn't it?" She pulled her arm out of his grasp.

"No, it's because finding Charlie is a lost cause that will surely end in your death."

"What's the big deal? The curse will pass on to another Grimm, and you can be free of me and go on to choose to help or not help the next Grimm."

Jared looked taken aback. He leaned against his car and crossed his arms. "Maybe I don't want to help another Grimm."

"Maybe I don't want your help, either, then. If you won't help me, then I'll find someone who will," she threatened him.

He snorted. "Who?"

"I don't know—there's got to be other Fae out there in this world who would be willing to help a Grimm."

Jared's face went red in embarrassment, and he started to stutter. "Uh, about that?"

"J-a-r-ed." She dragged out his name.

"There may be someone. I'll have to think about it." He got in his car without another word and drove off into the night.

Thirteen

She was having a nightmare. Reid was in her room, standing over Nan. Threatening to turn her into copper. He kept stroking Nan's face, taunting her. Mina was frozen in her dream state and couldn't move. Nan disappeared, and Reid slowly morphed into Temple. His voice filled the room and echoed into her unconsciousness. He reached a gold-dusted hand toward her, and she tried to evade his touch but was still frozen. Her breath came in gasps as he touched her face, and she could feel herself start to change and become gold. She looked at her hands and they were gold, but she could still move.

"Don't forget your promise," he whispered, then disappeared into the darkness, laughing at her.

The dream changed again, and she saw Charlie locked up in a golden cage, curled up in a small ball.

She called his name, and he sat up in confusion. Then his face lit up when he saw her, and he ran to the bars. Charlie held out his hand for her to grab him, but he was too far away.

"I can't! I don't know how to save you, Charlie. I don't know how to get over there." His hands dropped to his side, and she could see the disappointment etched in his small face. But then it was replaced by a look of fear. He pointed behind her, and she turned to see a wall of fire erupt around them. They both were trapped within its fiery grasp, and the fire raced between them, separating them both now by fire and the golden bars. There was someone else there. She could make out a male body lying on the floor, and she knew he was dead.

"NOOOO!" she yelled.

She woke up, breathing hard. The dream felt real—had she really seen Charlie? She lay in her bed and willed herself to go back to sleep so she could dream of her brother again and gain a clue as to how to save him. Sleep eluded her, and after she lay in bed for two hours, no more dreams came. She threw on a pair of blue shorts and a white T-shirt, and ran to the bathroom to quickly brush her teeth and run a brush through her hair without looking at it.

The wood floor was cold on her bare feet, and she paused when she heard voices coming from the kitchen. Quickly, she opened the door to the kitchen and was greeted by the sight of her mother and Jared sitting calmly at the kitchen table, chatting amicably. Mina froze with her hand on the doorknob. Her eyes went to her mother in disbelief and back to Jared.

He was dressed in the same clothes from last night and he looked like he hadn't slept, but that didn't take away from how handsome he looked. Never before had Jared shown any interest in getting to know her family. Did her mother know she was talking to the same Jared who had kidnapped her last year? No, if she did, she would probably demand that he leave the house…immediately.

Mina waited a few seconds, but nothing happened. Sara was oblivious to the internal battle her daughter was facing. Sara saw Mina come in, and she cleared her throat and motioned to Jared with her hand.

"Um, sweetie. This is Jared, and, uh…Terry sent him over to fix the shutters on the house."

Mina stared at her mom before giving a cursory glance at Jared, being careful to keep her face neutral.

"Oh," she responded.

"Now, I know this is sudden, but Terry assured me that he's a good worker, and if she trusts him, then so do I."

"How nice." Her mouth felt dry, her words forced.

Jared's eyes narrowed in thought as he leaned on the back legs of the kitchen chair, teetering on the brink of teenage rebellion. It was obvious that he knew something was up, even if her mother didn't. But Jared replied in a formal tone, "Nice to meet you…uh?"

"Mina," she answered irritably, knowing that he was only playing a part.

"What an odd name. Is it short for something?" he taunted her, knowing full well what it stood for.

"Yeah, a fat lip."

Wrong answer, because she heard a gasp from her mother, and Sara stood up.

"Now, Mina, apologize at once to our guest."

"Mom, look at him. Doesn't he even look remotely familiar?" Mina hinted.

Sara turned to stare at Jared with bewildered eyes and shook her head. "No, sorry, honey. Is he supposed to be familiar? I don't know—lately my mind has been pretty muddled. Can you show him the house…please?"

Mina rolled her eyes and held the door open for Jared to precede her into the hall, but not before she snatched an apple out of the fruit dish on the counter. When they had walked out of earshot, she snapped at him,

"Great, just great! Now you're brainwashing my mom."

He looked at her, confused. "I didn't do anything."

"Riiiight. What in the blazes are you doing here?"

"I started thinking about last night and what you said, and I realized that I may have acted—what happened to your hair?"

"Huh?" Her hand went to pat it, and it was still there.

Jared motioned with his fingers to her forehead, and she ran to the large hall mirror and gasped in shock. There was a whole lock of hair starting from her forehead that ran past her shoulders, and it was gold.

"I-I thought it was a dream," she whispered, fearing to touch it.

"What dream?"

"I dreamed about the Fae, about Reid and Temple and...and my brother. He was in a golden cage, and there was fire everywhere. He touched me in my dream, and now this." She swallowed and turned to Jared. "What do I do now?"

He stood there, looking at her in disbelief. "I can't believe it. You can do it?"

"Do what?"

"Do you understand what this means?" He was getting angry, and reached forward and grabbed her forearms.

"No, I don't know what it means, except that I'm scared."

"I—I'm sorry. I was wrong, and this proves it." He touched her hair in wonder. "If anyone can finish all of the quests and break the curse, it's you. And you're right—just because I can't help you with the Stiltskin, doesn't mean someone else can't. The old broads are going to hate me for this...well, they already hate me, but they will be very interested in this new development."

"Who?" she said impatiently.

Jared ignored her and headed down the hall to the front door. "Come on, let's go."

"Go? Go where?"

"To the old biddies. It's time to stir up the henhouse."

Fourteen

Jared led her outside to his motorcycle. She looked up at the house and the broken shutters he was supposed to fix. "What about the shutters?"

He turned toward the house and snapped his fingers, and the shutters reattached themselves to the house magically.

"And the front porch." Mina wasn't letting him out of his ruse that easily. Jared leaned toward the porch and barely looked at it before the step was fixed.

"Can we go yet?" Jared was chomping at the bit.

"The house needs painting."

"Done, now get on," Jared demanded.

Mina looked up, and the house was a pristine sparkling white.

He grinned and helped Mina put her helmet on, even going so far as to move her braid off her shoulder.

She looked up at the cloud-filled sky and frowned. Jared noted her look. "Trust me, I won't let a little rain ruin our parade."

She gave him a shocked look. "Trust a Fae? Never. But you'd better keep me dry, or next time it's the bus for us both."

He grinned, showing his white teeth, and flicked his visor down. Mina swung her leg over the back of his motorcycle and didn't know where to place her hands. This wasn't the first time she had ridden with him, but every time it was the same discombobulated feeling of what to do with her hands. She quickly got over it when the motorcycle roared to life. She wrapped her hands around his body to hold on as he sped toward the gate. He didn't slow down to enter the security code but sped up the closer they got.

Her heart thudded loudly and she squealed, thinking they would crash right through it, but it was all for nothing. At the last second, because of Jared's Fae power, the gate opened, letting them dart through. Jared laughed at Mina's scream and did nothing but go faster, making her squeeze him even tighter.

It was a twenty-minute drive before he pulled up to an old recycling plant on the waterfront. The building was a faded pea green, with the words *Green Mill Recycling Center* barely legible. The windows were boarded up, and even the doors had chains on them, deterring unwanted visitors. She headed toward the front door, but paused when Jared passed her and headed around back.

Fable

Jared searched around in the piles of "to be recycled bins" until he found the metal entrance door to a cellar. This door, unlike the others, wasn't chained or boarded up. It was sealed with a metal disc. The disc itself was bronze, with a sun and moon engraved on it. Ancient lettering was scrawled around the edges. He reached down, placed his palm upon the emblem, and whispered something unintelligible. Seconds later the seal glowed, then unlocked.

Jared grinned, opened the doors that led into a dark stairwell, and beckoned for Mina to enter. "Ladies first."

Mina hesitated. "Uh, age before beauty."

"Grimms never win."

"Prince before pauper."

"Oh, fine. Just don't say chivalry is dead. 'Cause you had your chance." He went down the steps first, stepping confidently over the plastic bottles and cardboard containers.

"Do you have a flashlight?" she asked, feeling uneasy.

"You're not scared of the dark, are you?"

"No, it's not the dark that scares me. It's the unknown...*and you*," she whispered.

He wasn't supposed to have heard the last two words, but he did. He turned on his heels quickly to face her, making Mina stumble on a glass bottle and skid into him. He deftly caught her against his chest, and when she struggled to remove herself from his grip, he didn't let go at first.

"Careful," he said. Pushing her back away from him roughly, Jared reached down, picked up a glass Coca-Cola bottle, and closed his eyes. A few seconds later a bright light emanated from inside the bottle. "Here you go. It will only last for a few minutes, but it should help chase the scary monsters away...including me."

Mina took the glass Coke bottle from Jared and stared at it in wonder. It was beautiful, a treasure, and it indeed lit up the passageway quite nicely. Walking with it, she could feel soft warmth coming from the bottle, but it never once burned her.

"It's right up here." He led them another twenty feet before he came to a dead end.

"There's nothing there."

"Aren't you the observant one," he replied sarcastically. "I bet you could always find Waldo, too. Now, bring the bottle closer so I can see."

She complied, and Jared reached into his back pocket and pulled out a small metal box. He selected two odd-shaped objects and inserted them into a miniscule hole in the wall. She could hear a few clicks of metal on metal.

"What are you doing?" she asked.

"Since I don't have a key to this fine establishment, I'm picking the lock."

"But you just used magic on the other lock. Why can't you do that on this one?"

"Because the other one was a magic lock, and this one isn't. It's a regular Schlage five-pin, so stop talking and let me concentrate...or would you rather do the lock picking?" He held the lock picks out to her.

Mina shook her head but asked, "If we are going to these people for help, why don't we just knock and use the front door?"

Jared's shoulders hunched in guilt. "Because I never knock. I shouldn't have to knock."

"So you just do this for your own enjoyment."

"Yes, and to see the look on their faces when I get the better of them." He grinned at Mina, and under the glow of the Coca-Cola-induced light, he looked stunning. So handsome that she almost forgave him for wanting to give up on finding her brother.

"A-ha!" The lock clicked, and he doused the light. Jared reached behind him and grabbed Mina's hand, and opened the door silently. A soft glow filled the passageway, and they entered a large library. Jared pushed the bookcase door they'd just entered through closed without a click.

There was a fire burning in the fireplace on the far wall, and the lounge chairs looked warm and inviting. One of them was currently occupied.

Mina watched as an arm reached out to take a teacup from a side table and disappeared behind the back of the chair. A few seconds later the cup was replaced, and the shuffle of a newspaper could be heard; the reader had not noticed their intrusion.

Something warned her to not say a word, mostly because Jared had been existentially quiet since they'd entered this room. He got Mina's attention with a wave of his hand and gestured to the west side of the room with his head. She turned to Jared and poked him in the arm, hard.

He cringed and dropped his shoulders, refusing to look at her. She pinched him harder until he turned around and swatted at her hands.

"We're breaking into someone's house?" She mouthed the words dramatically, and then hit him on the top of the head.

He tried to shush her with his hands, and then made a sheepish grin and nodded.

Mina scrunched up her face and raised her hands as if to strangle him, but got herself in check. *Why?* she motioned with her hands.

"Because you asked for help," he whispered, while never taking his eyes off the occupant in the chair.

"We are trespassing, and we're going to get caught, or worse, thrown in jail," she hissed quietly into his ear.

"Nah." He moved over to the far end of the room by two double doors next to a table with a large vase.

"Hello, Jared. Nice to see you again. Remember what happened the last time you tried to sneak into here?" The eloquent voice belonged to a woman.

Fable

Jared froze and rolled his head back to look at the ceiling, like a teen who'd just been chastised. "Yes," he grumbled.

Mina jumped at the voice and bumped the table. The vase on it teetered precariously and then toppled over before either one of them could catch it. Mina gasped as it crashed to the floor and shattered. Her head snapped to the occupant in the chair, and she heard a long, drawn-out sigh.

"Jared, Jared, Jared. Whatever am I to do with you? I fear that you will never learn." The paper was tossed lightly to the side, and the woman stood up to address them both. She was familiar. It was her music teacher, Mrs. Colbert.

"Mrs. Colbert?"

Mrs. Colbert looked perturbed that Jared had brought her here, and she stepped quickly over to the Fae prince and placed her hands on her hips.

"What do you think this is, a public library? You can't be coming and going here as you please. You do not have permission to be here, and you weren't supposed to bring her here, either. You, Fae prince, are ruining everything. Just because you did us one good deed does not mean the past is easily forgotten."

The door opened, and another woman peeked into the library. "Constance, there has been another development."

Mina was confronted with a woman who looked extremely familiar but at the same time foreign. There were enough similarities to give her doubt. The height, the dark brown eyes,

131

the tone of voice, but she was missing the wrinkles, the gray hair at her temples, and her thick and terrible accent. But it wasn't until the woman recognized Mina, let out a squeak of fear, and slammed the door that she knew she was right.

A few seconds later the door reopened, and Mrs. Wong stood before her.

"Mrs. Wong?"

Mrs. Colbert rolled her eyes and motioned to the woman. "Drop it, Mei—the prince let the cat out of the bag."

"Mrs. Wong, what's going on here? Are you one of them?"

Mei Wong's soft brown eyes closed as she took a deep breath and slowly let the glamour drop. There was only a faint shimmer of the air around her, and the old Chinese woman Mina knew and loved was replaced by a small woman with big beautiful eyes and skin the color of warm chocolate.

Hurt. Anger. Betrayal. All of those emotions ran through her, causing a disjointed symphony of pain. Mina unconsciously took a step back when the woman's hand reached out to touch her shoulder.

"Don't!" Mina whirled to confront Jared. "And you, you knew, didn't you? You've known all along that they were Fae."

Jared had crossed to stand by the window, letting the light filter through across his skin, giving him an otherworldly appearance. He tilted his head and studied her thoughtfully. "Are you saying you didn't?"

"I...uh. I don't know."

Fable

"You can't be that naïve. Didn't you know you would have one? They're the ones responsible for bringing the house to you. All Grimms have a babysitter." He shrugged and pointed to the prim and proper Mrs. Colbert. "They're not much good for anything else."

Mrs. Colbert's pink lips pinched together, and her eyes narrowed in anger. "Young prince, we are not babysitters. We are a collective Guild of Fae dedicated to the peaceful co-existence between Fae and non-Fae. We strive to keep the balance by protecting the Grimms."

Jared flashed his white teeth at Mrs. Colbert in challenge and bowed. "Oh, pardon me," he announced slowly, "your Orderliness."

"Now, hear me—" she began.

"Stop!" Mina yelled, her world once again crumbling beneath her. "What do you mean, you protect the Grimms?" She turned on Mrs. Wong, her words like daggers. "You've never protected me. Not from Claire, not from the wolves or the Reaper. If you are my protector, then why didn't you tell me about my father, about the curse, about the Story? You could have warned me."

"We watch, we guide, but we never ever interfere. But we broke that promise when your brother was born, and we've been trying to fix it ever since."

"Charlie! What does this have to do with Charlie? What did you do?" Mina began to pace frantically, keeping as much distance as she could between herself and the Fae. She should have known, should have seen the signs. They were there. Like the magic tea Mrs. Wong gave her that healed her injuries, everything pointed to the obvious, but she refused to believe it. Chose not to believe it.

"We will explain everything, but I think we need to have a seat. This could take a while. Come." She opened the white double doors and motioned down the hallway. "Follow me."

Mina hesitated at first, chewing on her bottom lip in indecision. She needed answers, and they had them. She dutifully walked after the female Fae, and Jared fell in line behind her. Mrs. Colbert...or as Mei called her, Constance...turned and in short, clipped words told him off.

"No, Jared. You may be our prince, but you do not rule over us. Where we go, you cannot follow."

He glared at her. "Don't you think I deserve some answers, too?"

She shook her head. "When you haven't earned those answers? I think not."

His mouth thinned into an irritated grimace, and he looked toward Mina before shrugging and walking over to the vacated chair. He made a big show of moving it loudly across the room and sitting in it while plopping his shoes on a white coffee table. He had a smug look on his face, and called out in a commanding tone. "Well, if you are to keep me waiting, at least fetch me something to drink."

Fable

Constance closed the door with a firm click. Mina highly doubted that Jared would be receiving that drink anytime soon.

She followed the woman who was her teacher and wondered at all of the things that had led up to this moment. Mei Wong followed a few steps behind them as they traveled the plush carpeted hallway. Her head was lowered and her steps slow, as if the Fae woman was trying to keep out of sight.

Feeling sorry, and somewhat responsible, Mina slowed to walk by her long-time friend. "So is your name even Mei? What about Ken? Are you two even married?"

She shook her head, her voice soft and melodic, unlike the clipped accent she favored. Upon closer inspection, her Fae protector didn't look that much older than Mina's own mother.

"It's Meira, or Mei for short, and yes, we're married." Her cheeks flushed, and her eyes twinkled mischievously. They stepped into a golden elevator and pushed the one-gemmed button. The doors closed, and instead of the elevator going up or down, it stayed in one place. The air crackled around them.

Mina kept stealing glances at the smiling Mei when it hit her like a ton of bricks.

"It was you, wasn't it? You wanted the Story to find me! You posted the pictures of me on your restaurant. You gave me magic tea. And your accent was terrible, by the way."

Mei looked around in panic.

Constance turned to Mei with her hands on her hips. "Mei, you didn't? You know better than to get involved too soon. You wait until we know for sure."

"Constance, forgive me, but the Story was bound to find her. No matter how many times we moved and I changed forms, and Sara changed schools, *he* always found her. The Story has always been particularly attracted to *my* Grimm. I knew despite her being a young girl that she would be the next one chosen. My Mina will be the one to break the curse. Just you watch and see." Mei grinned widely and winked in Mina's direction.

"This conversation is not over with, Mei. That was a serious breach of protocol."

The doors opened again, and they were in a large, circular white room filled with mirrors of all kinds: small mirrors, ornate mirrors, and mirrors larger than a pickup truck.

"Here we are." She smiled proudly and waved her hands around. "I know it's not much to look at and we run a small operation, but I think the Guild is something any Grimm would be proud of—well, I at least hope so, since you are the first one who has ever been here."

Mina walked around the room of mirrors and could catch a faint glimpse, or shadow, of activity in each of them.

"What are they?"

Mei walked up and gently stroked the silver edge around the closest mirror. "It's our looking glass. We can keep tabs on all of the Grimms. See, here's yours—uh, I mean mine." She

Fable

pulled the small handheld mirror off the hook on a wall and handed it to Mina.

At first it was filled with fog, and then the fog thinned to reveal a picture of Mina holding a mirror in a room surrounded by mirrors. She looked up and looked around her for a camera or to find whatever magical object was recording her and projecting her image onto the handheld mirror. The Mina in the mirror looked around the room at the same time.

"So there's a mirror for every Grimm." There couldn't be this many Grimms out there...or could there?

"Well, yes, there are more than you think. There is a mirror for every Grimm and a GM assigned to them...see. But the Story only chooses one at a time, so we keep track of all of them just in case. Even the distant cousins and the in-laws." She turned the mirror in her hands so Mina could see the name engraved on the back of the mirror. Her small handheld mirror had Meira's name etched in beautiful cursive letters. Mina put her handheld mirror back on the stand, and something in the next mirror over caught her attention. She snatched it off the shelf and walked away from Meira and Constance. It only took a few seconds for the image to clear up, and a perfect view of her mother vacuuming a house filled the glass. Without thinking, Mina flipped the mirror over to read the name on the back.

Terrylin.

"Terrylin." She whispered the name out loud. It sounded familiar, and then it clicked. "Terry! Terry is my mom's," she announced confidently.

"Yes." Constance frowned slightly. "She's your mom's GM. Although she didn't pick the most original alias."

"GM. You keep saying that," Mina said.

"Yes, Terry and Meira are your Fae Godmothers."

"You mean she's my fairy godmother, like in the movies."

"No, we are not all fairies, although there are a few fairies who have joined our Guild. We're a group of free Fae. Meira is a brownie, Terry is a house elf, which is why she prefers the cleaning business, and I'm a muse. We are many races united under one cause, and that is to help and guide the Grimms."

"Where's Charlie's?" Mina demanded. "I want to see Charlie's mirror."

Constance and Mei looked uncomfortable, and neither one spoke. "You can't see the dead, Mina."

"Oh, come on. I know that he's not dead."

Mei rushed forward to lay a comforting hand on Mina. "Sweetie, the mirrors can't see into the spiritual realm."

She brushed off Mei's hand and turned on them. "But he's not dead. A Stiltskin told me so."

"A Stiltskin!" both women said in unison.

"When did you meet a Stiltskin?" Mei asked.

"Not one, two." Mina tossed the Grimoire on a white marble table, and Mei opened up the book and looked at the last page thoughtfully. "I took care of this one. The other one has my brother."

"Well, that explains the mirrors not being able to find him. They can't see beyond this plane." Mei looked to Constance with a hint of relief in her voice.

But Constance was more concerned with something else. "Please tell me you didn't make a bargain with the other one. Please, Mina, no."

"I—I did, and I would do it a hundred times over if it meant I could save my brother."

Constance looked to Mei with worry in her eyes. "Well, this changes things, doesn't it?"

"Changes what?" Mina asked.

"Well, Sara is already wearing a Forget-Me-Not charm. We gave it to your mother to help her forget Charlie...permanently."

"Why would you do that? Why would you make my mother forget my brother?" Mina choked out.

Constance turned and gently took Sara's mirror out of Mina's hand and placed it back on the wall. "Child, listen to me, and listen to me well. Your mother has endured more than most. She's protected you as much as she could, and she's already lost your father. And after your brother, we didn't think she would pull through. We decided it was best to construct the charm so she could survive and be there for you. Right now you are more important than Charlie."

"You sound just like Jared," Mina said accusingly.

Constance frowned at Mina. "There are times when the wisdom of our banished prince surprises even us. But in this case, he's wrong. You made a deal with a Stiltskin, a deal sealed in blood, that only blood can break."

"So you'll help me? You'll help me save Charlie?"

"There's only so much we can do to help you, child. But know this—we are not doing this to save Charlie. We are doing this to save you. Because if you cannot obtain what the Stiltskin wants, you will become his slave...forever."

Fifteen

Mina thought time had stopped. As the world around her continued to move forward, her mind raced a mile a minute as the gravity of what the Godmothers had told her sank in. Her heart slowed, her vision became blurry, and she realized she was going to faint. But Mei grasped her arm and helped calm her down. Mei and Constance decided to get Mina walking, and they gave her a tour of the facility. They took her out of the room of mirrors and passed down a flight of stairs into a garage of sorts. It was a shop filled with male Fae working on all kinds of different projects. She could see some building an elevator like the one they had previously come down. One corner was alight with sparks, and Mina could see a centaur holding an arc welder.

"It's unbelievable what they are able to create when they have access to this world's machines and tools. The Fae have been dying to come over here just to have access to the

Internet." Constance stopped in front of the workroom and let Mina watch a dwarf sit down before a computer and print out a schematic for a design that a faun was working on.

"It has elevated all of their own projects and inventions. Technology on the Fae plane doesn't exist. It can't exist. Only magic or charmed items. So our facility also is a home to inventors, machinists, and Fae scientists. Who knows what one of them will discover when they combine their magic with your technology? The possibilities are endless."

Constance beckoned to Mina, and continued the tour down another hallway and pointed out a large indoor greenhouse. It was Mei who pointed excitedly and waved at a short man in the middle of a row of tomatoes. It was her husband, Ken Wong. He, too, looked different without the glamour. His skin was darker than Mei's, and his eyes had a gold tint to them. He looked quite happy and at home working in the gardens.

Mina knew then she wouldn't have to worry about her family friends. It was obvious they had people to help take care of them.

They passed through another set of double doors, and Mei pointed out the living quarters, the school, the watcher stations, the training stations, and finally the cafeteria.

"We are much more than just an organization. We help not only the Grimms but all of the Fae who have lost their way in this human world and can't adjust. We teach them about this

Fable

world, help them study it, and have them learn a trade so they can survive peacefully."

Constance opened another door, and they entered a large gathering area filled with Fae of all sizes, colors, and shapes. They were eating at long tables filled with food that smelled heavenly. When they saw Mina, the bustling stopped, and every one of them stared. After a few seconds, a furry cat about knee-high came up and pressed against Mina's leg, looking for affection.

Her hand immediately went to pull him off, but she changed her mind, and she decided to bend down and pet it instead. There was a large sigh, and the silence was broken as Fae after Fae began to clap and call her name. Mina's hand couldn't help but stroke the small furry head pressing into her knee. She looked down to see that it had disappeared, but her hand was still gripped in a headful of fur.

"Whoa!"

Hearing her confusion, the small cat reappeared briefly...only to change again into a dog, then a goat, and finally a squirrel that decided to run up her pant leg and settle on her shoulder.

"I see that you've made friends with our resident Baldander."

"What's a Baldander?" Mina asked, trying to hold still under the onslaught of the squirrel's curious hands.

"I think it's pretty obvious. That." Mei chuckled.

Mina reached up to try to pull it off, but it disappeared again and moved to her other shoulder.

"They're extremely rare. Give him a moment, and he'll settle down and stop shifting and disappearing on you. He's just excited to meet you and that you see him."

"Can't everyone see him?"

"No, not everyone," Mei answered.

A small furry hand patted her cheek in affirmation, and she could feel him settle down on her shoulder. He started petting her head as if she was his pet.

Constance motioned for them to continue on through the kitchen, and as she passed through the Fae, she could feel a few of them gently touch her arm, wish her luck, pat her on the back, all while the Baldander rode her shoulder, chittering in excitement.

"I'm not a pony—rides aren't free," Mina whispered under her breath.

The Baldander shifted into a mini Pegasus and flew around her head instead, still never leaving her vicinity.

They'd gone through the door and down another long hallway when she felt something odd. A change in mood, a coldness in the air. It was subtle, and maybe it was her imagination, but she felt like she was being watched. There in the corner was a large giant statue of a troll that blended in with the gray stone of the wall. It wasn't just blending with the color—it was actually half encased in the stone of the wall.

Fable

She paused and stared. It was so real-looking, very lifelike.

"Are you okay?" Mei asked.

"Yeah, I just—"

The troll opened its eyes focused on Mina. They were filled with such hate and anger that she began to tremble. Its gaze was powerful and intense, and she felt rooted to the spot, unable to move. The Baldander squeaked and disappeared off her shoulder to disappear who knows where.

Constance came between them, cutting off the troll's gaze with her body.

"Mina, it's okay. Don't look in his eyes. He can't hurt you unless you make eye contact. We're so used to him that we no longer see him, which is why he is disappearing into the wall."

Mina felt herself begin to regain control of her body and breathe easier. "What is he? Why is he there?"

Mei was the one who answered. "He was sent by the dark prince to destroy our headquarters over twenty years ago, and he's been frozen there ever since. It happened on an October morning. All but three of the GM headquarters were destroyed. He's been imprisoned since then."

"That's horrible."

"Would you rather we kill him?" Constance asked. "He can't do anyone harm there, and he's alive, which is more than I can say for the hundreds of Fae he killed years ago. Right now, he's frozen, and slowly he'll turn to stone."

"Are there more like him?"

145

Constance nodded. "The troll in Seattle is almost completely stone. He's under the Fremont bridge. Just don't look them in the eye, or you'll crumble under their hate."

Mina was able to pull her gaze away and follow the two Fae women back into a small office with round table. She sat in the closest chair and felt as if her feet were encased in stone. She looked around and saw that there was a giant map on the wall covered with glowing dots that she could only assume were Grimms, or persons of interest. Large pictures lined the wall, and she recognized them as her family tree. She saw her Uncle Jack, her father, and others—all strangers, but she could still see a familial resemblance.

Mei saw where Mina was staring and pointed out a blank spot proudly. "Your picture will eventually go here."

"What is this place?"

"These pictures represent all of the Grimms who have been cursed. It represents our call to action. Our call to help."

"Why are there so many?"

Mei look disturbed and refused to make eye contact with Mina.

Constance cleared her throat, and her hands fluttered nervously. "These portraits don't represent the living, Mina. These portraits represent the Grimms who have passed because of the curse."

"So you're saying that spot...that blank spot...is for my portrait—when I DIE! You people are disturbing." Mina shot up from the table and knocked over her chair, getting ready to make a beeline out of the door.

"Stop, Mina. You know more than anyone that you can't run from your destiny. Yes, many Grimms have come and gone. Most of them didn't make it past their first quest, mostly because they didn't have what you had. They didn't have the Grimoire. Have you not been studying the tales? Has Jared not been explaining things to you?" Constance asked.

"Yes and no," she replied grudgingly. "Can a Fae ever say anything outright without hiding it behind innuendos and half-truths? Sometimes I'm not even sure I should trust him."

"You're absolutely right—you can't fully trust him. But never mind that for now. The Grimoire came to you. You have an even bigger chance of beating this because you have figured out the Grimoire's secret. You're stronger than the rest."

Mina had to close her eyes and calm her heart and listen to them. She came here for help. She was probably the first mortal to ever step foot in the GM's headquarters.

"Okay, tell me about the Grimm curse, from your side."

Constance leaned forward and let her hands rest on the table in front of her. "Well, you already know that the Story prefers males. We believe this is because he thinks they're the stronger adversary. And the Story tends to choose the next Grimm from the closest living male relative, which is why it went from your grandfather to your uncle to your father. After your father died, the Story would have to pick another male

Grimm, so Sara thought it would go after some distant second or third cousin, and that you two would be free from the curse. But you know as well as I that a few weeks after your father's funeral, your mother found out that she was pregnant.

"Sara was extremely frightened and worried, and told Terry all of her worst fears of it being a boy, and the curse never leaving her family alone. Terry, using magic, was able to determine the sex of her unborn child. When your mother learned that she was carrying the next boy Grimm, she became hysterical, refusing to eat, sleep, and work. Finally, Terry, tired of watching and being unable to help her charge, begged us to intercede, and we did. We did something we promised we never would do. We intervened on an unborn Grimm. We cast a spell to make him invisible to the Story, to make the Story look elsewhere for his next Grimm."

"That's why Charlie is the way he is?" Mina gasped, and started to cry in relief. "I knew he was special, I knew he..." she sobbed, and Mei came over and hugged Mina and let her cry out all of her worries and frustrations.

"Yes, it is our fault that Charlie is different. He is harmless and of no interest to the Story, but the Story knew he had been duped. He always came back year after year to see if there had been a change. To see what had happened to his next Grimm. I think that is when he became interested in you, Mina," Constance said sadly.

Mei joined in excitedly. "He kept testing you when you were growing up, and your mom saw it and became frightened, and moved a lot. But I knew. I knew it would choose you."

"What about the house?" Mina asked.

"What about it?" Constance didn't seem worried.

"Where did that come from?"

"It's the same house the Grimm Brothers lived in hundreds of years ago. It's been invisible, hidden for years until the next Grimm needed it. We had to gather enough fairies and convince them to use a fairy circle to move it here, and each time it's moved it changes a little to fit the new surroundings. Your grandfather lived there, but your father just used it as his office. He refused to move your family there. He wanted to try to keep as normal a life as possible. And now it belongs to you."

Mina meditated on what she'd just been told. She had a house that was protected from Fae, a whole Guild of Godmothers that were of no help to her because they wouldn't fight, and a blank spot on their wall for when she died.

"What about the Grimoire? How did Jared and Teague get involved with the quests that originally started out between the Fates and the Grimm Brothers? Jared already told me that a sprite split the Fae book in two, creating the original Story and its doppelganger, the Grimoire, and that one is evil, the other good. But how do Jared and Teague fit in? When did they become so…attached?" Mina couldn't help but smile at her own joke.

Mei blushed and refused to look at Mina. "Well, that is a tender subject."

Mina could easily read between the lines. "It has to do with a girl, doesn't it?"

Constance interjected, "There's not a whole lot known about the Royals. A very secretive family, but there are always rumors. That something happened and someone cursed the princes into servitude to these books, and over the many years their personalities have changed and merged. One prince struggling to not become a slave to the book, while the other succumbed faster and became darker and more obsessed with power and the role of the tales."

It made so much sense now that she had more puzzle pieces and could finally see the whole picture. She began to feel sorry for Jared and his brother. "Is there nothing to be done to break their curse?" she asked.

"Oh, Mina. No wonder he chose to come to you. Only you would be worried about breaking someone else's curse over your own."

Mina sat down at the table and felt something brush against her calves before scrambling back into her lap. She didn't have the energy to push the Baldander off, and in fact was finding comfort in his nearness. It was soothing stroking his fur and thinking through all the new information she just learned.

Fable

Constance cleared her throat to get Mina's attention. "But we need to focus on your problem, not theirs. So back to the problem at hand. What kind of Stiltskin were they?"

"One was young, a teenager like me. The other was older. He looked like he just walked out of a comic convention."

"No, Mina, not what were they wearing—what was their element? What form did they work in? Was it tin, iron, bronze, silver?"

"Oh! Uh, copper. Reid kept changing everything to copper."

Mei looked relieved. "Copper means he was probably the youngest-born sibling. The one who you made a deal with…?"

"Gold," she answered excitedly. "Everything he touched turned to gold."

Constance let out a long sigh and rubbed her forehead wearily. "That's what I was afraid of. He's the oldest son, then, probably from the original family. If only you had met a nickel or bronze. We could have handled one of those—but gold? That goes back to the original Stiltskin family, to Rumple himself."

"Well, in that tale all the princess had to do to save her child was guess his name, so shouldn't it work the same way? He already told me his name. It's Temple."

"They've wised up, changed their bargains and deals. Names used to hold a great deal more power. I think our best bet is to try to do what he wants, although he will more than

151

likely try to trick you into becoming his slave either way. So the first order of business is, what did he want?"

All of a sudden, something told her not to tell them. A small voice warned her away from the GMs. If she told them she was going after the Fae book, they might refuse to help her, just like Jared. So, out of self-preservation for her quest, she lied. "He didn't say yet. He wanted me to cross over to the Fae world first, and then he would find me and tell me what my task is."

"Are you kidding me? There can only be one reason he wants a Grimm to cross over. He's going to send you after the Royal Family," Mei said nervously.

"You're right. You can't do it. I doubt you could get to the palace without getting killed. So you only have one other choice. You have to kill Temple first," Constance said.

Sixteen

"No, no way. Do you see what he did to me!" She pointed to her golden stripe of hair. "And this was when I was sleeping. Uh-uh. Not happening."

"That is exactly why you have to kill him. You are the only one who can. You've already started connecting to the Fae plane," Constance said.

"I have?"

"You did, in your sleep. The Fae plane is somewhere between the physical plane and the spiritual one. Jacob and Wilhelm were the only Grimms to successfully go there of their own free will. No other human has done it since. But you can. Temple didn't come to you in your sleep. You went to him, or at least connected with him in a dream, and the power that continues to grow around you helped make it real."

"So how do I do it again?"

Both of the women looked at each other and shrugged. "We don't know."

"Jared brought me here promising that you would help me," she cried out.

"We want to help you, but this is a gift we know very little about," Mei said.

"But if you can get there once, you can get there again. You may have to wait until you solve more quests. It's not just the Story who is growing stronger and more powerful the more quests you complete. You are as well. So maybe in time you will have more control over this ability. But at the moment we don't know what else to do."

"Is there no other option? That can't be the only way for a human to cross over. What about all of those tales about the Fae stealing children?"

"Children are smaller and take less energy, but it takes a very strong and powerful Fae to cross over with an adult human. Most are barely strong enough to come by themselves. I assume you asked Jared." Constance looked at Mina carefully, already knowing the answer.

"Of course, he won't go to the Fae plane. I don't understand why."

"It's because it is more dangerous for him to cross over than it would be for you. Jared's been banished, and if he goes back, he risks losing his life."

"I wish he would tell me these things," Mina fumed.

Fable

Mei kept chewing her lip in thought. "Maybe if you had a seam ripper?"

"Is that a small silver tube thing?" Mina asked, feeling her heart race with excitement.

"Why, yes, a wizard gave one to each of the Fates. Do you think you know where one is?" Constance asked.

"I think I know someone who has one."

When Mei took Mina back to the library again, Mina was completely discouraged. She had more questions than answers. The Godmothers said they would try their European contacts and find out what they could about jumping. That's what they were calling it. Jared was sleeping in the armchair by the fireplace and didn't stir at the sound of their entrance.

Mei held Mina's hand and whispered encouragement to her.

"Mina, I truly believe you will be the one to break the curse. You have something that none of the other Grimms had." She looked toward the sleeping Jared.

"Jared?"

"Never before has the Grimoire shown its human side. There's something special about you, Mina. Something that I saw years ago, something that our young prince saw. Trust in that."

Mina turned to stare at the sleeping Jared and felt consumed with conflicting emotions and questions. The first day she found the Grimoire and was attacked by Grey Tail, Jared could have just stayed within the book, but he interfered. He showed his true self to her, and on numerous times before. Yes, he wasn't always truthful, but he was protecting himself and his family. Wouldn't she do the same if she was in his shoes?

A soft click of the door told her that Mei had left the library, but it was followed by the soft clicking noise of nails on the floor. Mina grinned, knowing what was running toward her. But the Baldander didn't jump onto her; instead, the invisible fur ball jumped onto a sleeping Jared, who jumped up and hollered in alarm.

"Holy mother of fate, what is that!" He flung his arms wide, and a knife instantly appeared in his hands, ready to attack.

The Baldander chirped loudly and became visible in its squirrel form. It jumped in front of Mina protectively and shifted into a large cat.

Mina laughed at the two squaring off against each other.

Jared tried to shoo the cat, but it didn't budge. In challenge, Jared, who because he had royal blood could shift at will, did just that. He shifted into a large dog and growled at the cat.

The cat morphed into a snarling wolf. Jared morphed into an even bigger wolf. The Baldander shifted into a tiger. Jared shifted into a lion. Back and forth they went, challenging each other, until the library was filled with a giant dragon and large troll.

"Enough! Down, boys, you're both very powerful. I get it."

Fable

Jared was the first to morph back into his human form, and he seemed slightly embarrassed to have let the small Fae get the better of him.

"Sorry, but what is that?" He pointed in disgust at the dragon, which had morphed down to be pocket-sized and was flapping its wings as if it had won the rumble.

"It's a Baldander."

"No way! I thought they were extinct."

The little dragon turned and blew what looked like a fiery raspberry at the Fae prince.

"I guess they're not, and I don't think it cares one lick that you're a prince." She giggled. The dragon flew up and settled in the crook of Mina's hood, and quickly became invisible again.

"I don't trust that thing," Jared shot back.

"Relax, I find him quite cute. Isn't that right, Ander?" She held up a finger and felt the invisible dragon rub its face against her.

"Great, you've named it, now you're gonna want to keep it. But I'm telling you that thing better be house-trained." He turned to the bookshelf and began to pull open the book to open the hidden exit door.

Mina felt Ander leave her shoulder but didn't let Jared know he was missing. She saw Constance's teacup float mysteriously above Jared's head. She clapped her hand over her mouth to contain the laughter. A second later the cup turned over, spilling lukewarm tea on Jared's unsuspecting head.

"Oh, it better not have just peed on me!" he screamed.

The teacup clattered to the ground as Ander released it. Jared saw the cup and glared at the dragon. An instant later he turned and jumped into the air. Morphing into a hawk, he took off chasing the miniature dragon around the room.

Mina pushed the door open and headed out the cellar doors, knowing that Ander would be just fine against a quick-tempered Jared. She hoped that Jared would come out with his ego still intact.

It had grown dark since they entered the recycling plant, and the night air was chilly on her bare arms. She walked over to Jared's bike, sat on the seat, and surveyed the surroundings. The river lined the east side of the building, and the road and the parking lot were overrun with weeds and old containers. On the west side was the edge of a forest, the evergreens that lined the edge of the forest looking like sentinels guarding the Fae Godmothers. So much had happened in such a short time, and she was just as confused as ever.

An intense prickling feeling ran up her back and tickled her fingers, followed by a familiar sound that pierced the night. Mina jumped off the bike, wary and alert. She scanned the dark forest, knowing that was where the sound came from—a very unique sound that she knew belonged to Stiltskin's bird. She watched the forest and at first saw nothing, but then a glow emanated from the darkness and grew brighter and brighter.

Fable

Mina pulled out the Grimoire, and it immediately turned into a bow and arrow. She notched the arrow and pulled back the string, and sighted on her target. The bird flew between the trees, alighting on one branch and then flying to another one a little closer. It continued the same pattern, as if trying to not startle her. Something felt different this time; she didn't feel any aggression from the bird. The giant golden bird stopped at the edge of the forest on a branch of the nearest evergreen. His long golden feathered tail almost touched the branch underneath him. Fire trickled from under his wings, as if the bird was made of fire and the feathers were holding the inferno in check.

The fire bird shifted back and forth on the branch, and she spun around, checking behind her for a hidden attack. Nothing. They were the only ones in the forest.

"Why are you here?"

The bird tilted his head as only a bird could and became more agitated.

She held up the arrow again and threatened the bird. "You do anything, ignite a single spark, and I'm having Kentucky Fried Chicken for dinner."

The bird screeched, and her body erupted in shivers, its call going through her bones. It really was a chilling sound. The bird bent its glorious head and began to peck at his tail feathers until he had pulled the longest feather off and held it in his beak. The bird opened his wings slowly and glided off the branch toward

Mina; he dropped the feather on the ground before her and circled back.

The firebird emitted one more piercing screech, and then it shot into the night, leaving a blazing trail of fire behind him. She watched the firebird and looked back at the gift it had left in parting. The feather was mysteriously still burning brightly. She waited to see if it would eventually burn out, but it didn't. Feeling brave, she picked up the gold feather and ran her fingers over the top, and felt its softness. Apparently being made of gold didn't change the texture of the bird's feather. The after-feather, or soft downy part of the feather, still flickered with fire, and even after she gave it a good shake, it continued to burn. She held her fingers as close as she could and didn't feel any heat. Finally, her curiosity getting the better of her, she touched the flame itself and felt nothing but coldness.

Why? What purpose did the firebird have in giving her a feather when it was obviously Stiltskin's pet? Stiltskin! Did he follow her here? Did he now know that this was the Godmothers' headquarters?

Gripping the feather, she ran back toward the cellar and was greeted by a perturbed Jared on his way up.

"Stupid hamster." He turned on his heels and yelled back into the darkness, "I hope you get rabies, you brat."

It didn't take a genius to figure out which Fae had won the challenge.

"Jared? I think the Stiltskin was here."

Fable

"What do you mean?"

"I mean, look at this." She held out the feather, and Jared studied the burning phenomenon and reached out to touch it experimentally.

"Huh? Cool," he intoned.

Mina wasn't taking it as laid-back as Jared. "His pet firebird appeared out here and gave this to me. Do you think he could be here as well? Did I lead the Stiltskin to the Godmothers?"

Jared stepped away from her and lifted his head to the night. Closing his eyes, he turned in each direction before turning back. "No, there are no other Fae beside the bird. Mina, I think he was trying to help you. I don't think it's a trap—I think it's a gift."

"Yeah, but what does it do?"

"I don't know. It's a phoenix feather. History has all kinds of rumors about them. Some say they can bring back the dead, regenerate, give you infinite riches like a philosopher's stone. But I can understand why this Stiltskin would want one. If he is obsessed with gold and has a golden phoenix, that would make him even more powerful."

"And this may be my only clue."

"Or a peace offering."

"Jared, I'm running out of time. Do you think the Stiltskin figured out I'm reneging on my deal? How long before he comes to collect me?"

"I don't know, but he won't get you without a fight. That you can count on."

"So you've decided to help me save Charlie?"

"No, I told you. You have to forget him and worry about yourself. I was hoping the Godmothers would help you find a way to break the deal you made with the Stiltskin." He reached for her hand and grabbed it, holding it firmly. His hand felt warm and strong, and sent shivers up her arm. "Mina, I'm doing things for you that I've never done for any other Grimm in history, and I don't know why. It worries me, the choices I keep making, and Ever's right. Maybe I am getting too involved, too close."

Her body went cold at his words, and she ripped her hand out of his. "What do you mean, you're getting too involved?"

He shrugged. "Look at us. The more I think about it, the more I realize I made a mistake."

"You're my Grimoire, for goodness' sakes. You are supposed to help me finish the quests! I realize that you're at odds with your family on this, but are you backing out now because of Ever? I realize that you have obligations and you can't always tell me what's going on, but I thought we'd gotten past that."

"What you're doing is committing suicide. You'll be unprotected in a land of Fae. Who knows where you'll appear there? It's too dangerous. I won't let you go there, even for Charlie."

162

Fable

She stood there in the cold night air. "I'll find a way to save him, Jared. Maybe Ever will help me."

Jared snorted. "Yeah, right. As if she can find her way back home. She can't even find her way to the nearest mall half the time."

"Well, the Godmothers said I would have to wait until I complete more quests and grow stronger, or use her seam ripper."

"You're saying Ever has a seam ripper."

"Yes," Mina said slowly.

"When did you see Ever cross over? Think carefully, Mina."

She was taken aback at the change in subject. "Last year she approached me when the Reaper had stolen the Grimoire and I didn't know where you were. She used this tube thing, and drew a circle and disappeared." Mina indicated with her fingers the size of the tube.

Jared was distracted and began to walk toward the parking lot. "It's a seam ripper, and only a few of them exist. It cuts right through both planes to create a temporary gate, but they are dangerous. Only the strongest of Fae are able to travel back and forth at will, and they become weakened almost to the point of death. Which is why a wizard developed the seam rippers to create gates for the Royals and the ruling Fates. Wherever a gate has been ripped open, it is weakened for a certain amount of time—that's how the lesser Fae get over here. But these...these

163

are gifts given to a handful of people, and she was not one of them."

He motioned for her to get on the bike. He started the motorcycle, and they were once again off into the night. Mina had no clue where Jared was taking her and was only slightly surprised when he pulled up to a small rundown motel. Jared flew off the bike, and stormed over to room number eight and pounded on the door. A few seconds later, Ever opened the door, wearing a cute gray dress, and smiled brightly at Jared...until she saw his expression. Then she cast an accusing look at Mina. Behind her, Mina could make out a sparsely decorated hotel room with a few books and a backpack on the bed.

Jared motioned with one finger for her to follow, and he walked briskly into Ever's room. Mina followed, keeping her head down as she entered the pixie's private domain. She felt terrible that the girl was sleeping in a motel. That was, until she closed the door and the glamour lifted. What once was a room with a single dirty bed with a broken lamp turned into a very large apartment filled with every plant imaginable. There were wide windows that gave the room a greenhouse effect. The dining room table and furniture were white, but the artwork and statues that decorated the home were filled with pixies.

Ever's face was pale, her eyes wide with worry, but she was still spunky enough to throw Mina a perturbed look before following her into the living room.

Fable

It was obvious from the way Jared didn't bother to look around the room that he had been there before.

"How could you, Ever?" Jared asked, his voice like ice.

"How could I what?" she snapped back.

"Why would you lie to me?"

"Do you know what he is talking about, Gimp, 'cause I sure don't?"

Mina was uncomfortable under Ever's scrutiny. She shrugged.

"This isn't about her, Ever. This is between you and me," Jared shot out.

She stood up, her eyes blazing. Her hair started to blow about her shoulders.

"No, it's not. It's always about her! There is no you and me—you've seen to that. Ever since she showed up, you don't care about me anymore."

"That's not true. It's complicated, and more so now that you can't be trusted. What deal did you make with the Fates? What deal did you make with my mother?"

"Who told you?"

"Who gave you a seam ripper?" he demanded.

Ever's eyes snapped up to glare at Mina accusingly and then went innocent when she looked up at her prince. They filled with tears. It was obvious that she loved him and had done something terrible.

165

"I left everything behind for you! I gave up everything so I could come over here to be with you. They helped me come over, and all I had to do was report back about you. It wasn't supposed to be like this." Her gaze traveled back over to Mina. "She was supposed to fail like the others, and then it could be like the old times again. You weren't supposed to really help her!"

"Give it to me!" Jared held out his hand to Ever.

Her back stiffened, and her shoulders rose. "No, I can't."

"Ever, you weren't meant to have one. Now, give it to me!"

"I—I won't. I can't. It's my only way back to visit my family. It's not my fault you've become soft-hearted and want to help the Gimps." She let slip the derogatory name the Fae called the Grimms.

"It's too dangerous for you to have one. How many times have you used it already, and where? Here? Mina's house?" Ever's head dropped, and she looked over at Mina guiltily. "Please don't tell me you've used it near her house?" Jared pointed to Mina.

"I had to," Ever squealed. "You were spending too much time with her, getting attached. We were afraid of losing you. I had to follow you both."

"Anything could have come through! We don't know what is roaming around here now. You probably even let in another Reaper."

She shook her head and held up her hand. "No."

Jared's fists were turning white from how tightly he was clutching them. Mina thought she could actually hear his knuckles pop from the strain.

"Ever!"

She bit the bottom of her lip in worry, and, finally realizing there was no other option, she got up and dug through her purse. Her hands were shaking, and Mina thought she heard a few sniffs come from the pixie's direction. Ever turned with her fist closed and held it out to Jared.

He snatched it out of her hand fast as lightning and bolted for the door. Her shoulders dropped and she nodded. Before grabbing the doorknob, Ever turned and spoke, her voice ringing with fear. "Please don't hold this against me, Jared. I did this for you. I did this for us."

Jared ran his hands through his dark hair and spun on her angrily. "No, you did this for you. I forget how selfish pixies are—they are unable to truly care about anyone other than themselves."

"You don't mean that."

"Then prove it. Prove that your race doesn't define who you are. Show me that you are not just like all the other pixies. That you care more about others than yourself."

Ever's beautiful eyes filled with tears, which she tried to blink away. Her head dropped to her chest, and she took a deep breath before closing the door.

Jared stared at the object in his hand and tucked it into his pocket before making eye contact with Mina. He smiled wanly, but the smile didn't reach his eyes; he looked tired, worn-out.

"Let's get you home," he said.

She didn't respond, just sat stiffly on the bike as he once again drove her home. This was becoming the night that would never end. When he once again pulled up to her house, he sat on his bike, immobile.

She got off the bike and stared at him. She knew then from the angry look in his eyes that he had no intention of ever helping her save her brother. He did all of that to take the seam ripper for himself, not to help her. He could just give her the seam ripper and she could go alone. He wouldn't have to even cross over and endanger himself.

Jared left her no other choice—she was going to betray him, betray what little trust they had gained. And once she finished her quest, she would deal with the repercussions then. She closed her eyes and opened her senses, willing the feeling of power to come to her. It did. She was living in a home made of Fae magic, close to a royal Fae prince. It was becoming easier and easier to recognize the lingering power that was always there, just on the edges. She remembered when she'd called out for help and Jared had answered. He didn't come because he wanted to; he came because she commanded him to help her. Now she was about to do the same thing.

"Jared, give me the seam ripper." She pushed all of the power into those words.

His eyes went wide in shock, and he backed away from her in horror.

"Mina! What are you doing?"

"Just as you are bound to the Grimoire, you are bound to me and my will. I command you to give me the seam ripper."

"Don't do this, Mina. You don't know what you're messing with. You can't trust Fae magic—you're not Fae." Even as he said the words, she could see that he was fighting with himself and the power of the command. His hand thrust into his pocket and gripped the seam ripper and pulled it out.

"I know what I am asking you to do, and I'm sorry that it has to be this way."

"Mina, don't make me do this!" Jared's eyes were pleading, his whole body struggling with inner turmoil as he fought the Fae magic. "Please," he called out.

The tears she had been holding back flowed freely. She was taking away his free will.

"If you do this, Mina, I won't forgive you!" He yelled out the words as he fell to his knees in pain, his fist flung out in front of her.

"I have to, Jared. There's something I have to do."

"NO...not like this." One by one his fingers uncurled to reveal the shiny silver tube. "You are breaking our trust."

"Jared, you never fully trusted me to begin with, and right now I have to save Charlie. When this is over, I can only hope you'll forgive me. But right now, I'm not asking for your permission or forgiveness."

Jared let out a painful grunt, and with a final act of free will he threw the seam ripper to the ground and crushed it under his boot. Pieces of it flew across the ground, scattering into the darkness.

Shock. Anger. Hurt. It all rushed over her and took control of her body. Her hand slapped Jared so fast across the face, she surprised herself.

Jared's cheek turned an angry red, and the muscle in his jaw twitched in anger, but he refused to look at her. Instead, his angry glare was directed at the darkness behind her.

"You could have chosen to go with me to help me," she hissed.

"I can't." He looked into her eyes to show her how serious he was. "*If* you go there, Mina, you'll be going there alone." Jared glared at her.

Seventeen

School was a torture. Nothing could make her happy. Jared was refusing to talk to her, and Ever was avoiding sitting at their lunch table. Mina kept staring at the clock on the wall in first period, always wondering how many minutes would pass before Stiltskin came for her. Could it be weeks? Months? Days? The Godmothers made it very clear that the magic of a deal in blood could very well be stronger than the power of her Grimoire, so she needed a Plan B. Another way to beat him if he came for her, 'cause she obviously had no way to cross over.

Someone called her name, and she came out of her daydream to stare into Brody's worried eyes.

"Are you okay?" he asked.

"Yeah, sure."

"Hey, I'm sorry about our triple date and—"

She held up a hand to stop him. "Please…don't mention it…really."

"We could try again, maybe this next Friday," he said hopefully.

"Uh, no, thanks. I think the trio has dissolved," she said, referring to their very empty lunch table the day before. Jared and Ever had been absent, and Mina didn't think she could sit by Nan and Brody for one more day without them.

The bell rang, and she darted from her chair and out into the hall, then headed to the music room, deciding it was better to get a detention for skipping a class so she could talk to Constance, er, Mrs. Colbert, in between classes. She followed a bunch of girls she didn't know into the choir room and decided to stick close to a tall brunette with hair down her back and a smattering of freckles across her pert nose. She wore a light blue shirt with a pink elephant on it.

She was listening to music on her iPod and was quietly humming to herself. Mina watched her stretch to her tiptoes multiple times while waiting in line, the sign of a dedicated dancer practicing at every opportune moment. She popped out an earbud, and Mina could hear the faint sounds of country music playing before the girl turned off her iPod and put it away. The line had moved, and it was their time to get music. The brunette picked up a music binder, and turned and handed one to Mina as well. She knew she had picked the right girl to shadow.

"Hi," the girl said softly. "First time in choir?"

"Yes, and after Mrs. Colbert hears me sing, it will probably be my last," Mina joked.

The girl laughed. It was soft and melodic. "I'm Melissa."

"Mina."

"Are you an alto or soprano?"

"Uh…what are you?" Mina asked.

"Soprano."

"Me, too," Mina lied.

"Then you can come sit by me and Bekah. We'll help you blend, and we'll poke you if you go off key," Melissa teased.

Mina followed Melissa to the second row and hesitated. She didn't want to sit this close to the front of the class. She would rather have sat in the back, but someone filed in behind her, and Mina was forced to keep moving.

Melissa pointed to the girls on either side of them. "That's Julianne, Makaylee, and, of course, Bekah." Each girl waved when she heard her name mentioned and smiled.

"Are you going to audition for the musical?" Makaylee asked.

"Musical?"

"Mrs. Colbert always picks a fairy tale. Last year it was *Princess and the Pea*, the year before, Rapunzel. I wonder what it will be this year?" Bekah wondered.

"I hope it's not *Red Riding Hood*," Julianne answered.

"Uh, definitely not."

"I'm sure there's a kissing scene." Melissa shuddered. "You never know who would get cast as the prince, and that could be very awkward."

All the girls nodded in unison, but there was a wishful look behind their eyes.

Mrs. Colbert walked into class and took her place behind the piano. She called out to the class and began to do warm-ups. Mina was altogether shocked by the voice that came out of the Fae teacher. Constance wasn't kidding when she said she was a muse. She could really sing, and it was obvious that the Fae loved singing. Her face lit up with joy, and she didn't notice the extra student sitting in on her class.

Music binders opened, and Mina watched Melissa's carefully to see what page they turned to and tried her best to hide behind the music. They were working on a piece from *Phantom of the Opera*, and Mina stopped singing to stare at Melissa. The teen girl had closed her eyes and was hitting every one of the notes with ease. Mina was slightly envious and tried to follow along, but her voice cracked, betraying that she was indeed an alto. Melissa opened her eyes and made a poking motion with her finger. Then she smiled widely and winked.

Mina found herself smiling back and thinking how she could see Melissa and Nan being great friends. Halfway into the second song, Mrs. Colbert finally noticed the new addition to her class. She froze for a second and then recovered beautifully. She raised an eyebrow in question at Mina but continued with the rest of class. She ended early and gave the final instructions about the auditions.

"You've heard that our musical has been announced. This year we are doing *Cinderella*. Auditions will be in three weeks after school in the main auditorium. Please come prepared with a solo piece to perform. That is all."

Since the class ended early, Mina had hoped the students would all disappear from the room, but that wasn't the case. With the excitement of the announcement of the musical, everyone wanted to stay and talk.

Mina excused herself and squeezed out of the row, and left the girls talking excitedly about the play.

"What are you doing here?" Mrs. Colbert asked, a forced smile on her face. "Is something wrong?"

"No, not really. It's just that a lot has happened since the other night. Jared destroyed the seam ripper, he's not talking to me anymore, and I haven't jumped or whatever in my sleep. I don't know what to do."

Mrs. Colbert took off her blue wing-tipped glasses and her glamour faded a little, making her look like the muse Constance more than ever. "Mina, listen to your heart. When the time is right, you'll know what to do."

"No, I don't. I'm too close. I can't find my way, and Jared's not helping me."

The students continued talking amongst themselves, and Mrs. Colbert sat on her piano bench and motioned to the music in front of her.

"Remember what I said about technology not working on the Fae world? Man-made things can't transfer over there. We don't know why—it just can't. It's a rule, a law of some sort that can't be changed. And just like that rule, another one always seems to surface in regards to stories."

She waved her hand over the sheet music, and the notes and lines began to merge and dance across the white paper. She began to play the piano, and the lines and notes formed a story. The more she played, the more the picture continued.

"With every tale throughout time, there are rules. A hero is given an impossible task." A knight appeared made of the notes on the white paper, sword in hand, bowing before a king. Then the drawing changed into the knight traveling through a dangerous forest alone.

"One that he is sure to fail, but along the way help comes from the most unexpected source." The knight helped three creatures, and they offered him a boon. "When the hero reaches an insurmountable obstacle, he forgets that he has allies who will come to help him. One by one the creatures in the story help the knight overcome his obstacles and traps, and he reaches his goal. And wins the princess's hand in marriage." She stopped playing, and the moving pictures turned back into plain sheet music. "Mina, we are not your only allies, and the Story, as you very well know, is not your only adversary. If the quests were easy, then the curse would have been broken long ago."

"But how do I know that this is even a quest?"

"Because it's the loophole of all Fae tales. Whenever you, the hero, get stuck, something or someone will magically aid you on your quest. That you can be sure to count on. The ending of the tale is still very much in your hands, but I wouldn't be surprised if you already have the answer and you just don't know it. Don't forget that the Fae prince is very much a servant of the Fae book. So they all have rules to follow."

Mina sighed in frustration. "So you're saying a furry woodland creature is going to come and help me?"

"Mina, all Fae are attracted to you. Help will come to you if it hasn't already."

She was about to tell her teacher about the mysterious phoenix feather gifted to her when the second bell rang. Mina looked up to see the next class filing in and pulling out music stands and opening violin cases. Constance's next class had arrived.

"Oh, I, uh. I'm late," Mina said sheepishly.

Constance pulled out a pink pad of paper and quickly wrote an excused tardy on her note, and handed it to Mina. "As much as I loved having you drop in today, try not to make a habit of skipping classes. Your education is extremely important."

"As important as my other job," Mina hinted.

Constance frowned. "No…yes. Oh, that's not the point. Get going."

Mina left and headed to her next class, which was gym. Oh, why couldn't she have skipped this period instead? Then again, it would have been a lot harder to pretend to play a stringed instrument than it was to slink into choir class. Since she had the pass, she took her sweet time heading to the gym, but came to a sudden halt when she turned the corner and saw him standing, staring at the school's trophy case. It was Temple.

His back was stiff. He wore a long gray suit jacket trimmed with gold buttons, and gray lambskin gloves.

"A lot of trophies. Too bad they're just pieces of plastic. Not worth anything. Unlike my prized collection." He turned to look at her and squinted his eyes in study. "You've been straying from your goal, and I've become impatient."

Mina spoke evenly. "They say that patience is a virtue."

"So is self-control, and I feel that mine may be slipping where your brother is concerned." He opened his coat and pulled out a small glass globe. He held it out in front of her, and she could see Charlie inside a gold cage, just like her dream. "I have heard some disturbing news. It seems my youngest brother has disappeared. You wouldn't have anything to do with that, would you?"

"Maybe he went on a spur-of-the-moment vacation."

Fable

"Maybe I have decided to change my mind about what I want. If you can't get the Fable, the Fae-plane book, then I want the Grimoire."

"No, you can't have it!"

"No one tells me what I can and cannot have," he hissed, and raised his fist and smashed it through the trophy case. The glass shattered and rained to the ground in pieces. He shook his hand and put it back down by his side. He had lost control and was on the verge of trying to regain it. Temple closed his eyes, and smoothed his vest and jacket back into place. "Be glad that I'm gracious enough to spare yours until our bargain is done. You have until tomorrow at midnight to give me one of the books, or your brother will die and you will take his place in my gilded cage. Don't disappoint me again."

He turned and strolled down the hall, his boots making a hollow clicking noise. Mina stared at the shattered trophy case and Temple's retreating figure, and felt her heart race. She needed to leave before someone came to investigate the disturbance. But something on the ground caught her eye; she stooped down and picked up something he had missed: a shard of gold-tinted glass with a single drop of Temple's blood on it. He must have unknowingly cut himself on the shard of glass, turning it gold.

A door opened, and she could hear the sound of feet quickly approaching. Mina slipped the shard into her jacket pocket and ducked around the corner just before Principal Hame appeared and yelled, "What in the blazes happened to the trophy case?"

Eighteen

She was out of options and desperate. Mina sneaked off to her locker and began to work on the combination. Of course, since she was in a hurry, her fingers wouldn't cooperate with her, and it took her three tries to get the correct combination before she heard the audible click and the locker opened. It was just around the corner from the trophy case, and she knew if she didn't get moving she would get in big trouble for skipping class. And she didn't think that saving the world from Fae was an acceptable excuse. In fact, she would probably end up in the school counselor's office if she tried that excuse.

The commotion was getting louder as more teachers came to investigate Principal Hame's verbal tirade against delinquents that destroy school property. And how he would find them and they would be expelled.

Come on, she mentally berated herself, and desperately dug around in her backpack for it. Her fingers brushed something

Fable

warm, and she snatched it out of her bag and slammed her
locker door a little too loud.

"Did you hear that? It's probably our delinquent now." His
voice got louder, and Mina could hear his footsteps drawing
closer to her.

She clutched the golden phoenix feather close to her breast
and tried the doorknob to the nearest classroom. Luckily, it was
unlocked and currently devoid of students. It took her a moment
to adjust to where she was because all of the shades had been
closed against the heat of the sun. She moved forward away
from the door and bumped into the familiar lab table. It was the
biology lab. This room always gave her the willies, as she
couldn't help but remember what had happened the last time she
was in this room. The creepy specimens in the lab's glass cases
had come alive. She moved to the corner of the room and
crouched down behind a tall file cabinet. Would they look in the
darkened classroom?

A moment later the door opened, and the light from the
hallway spilled into the room. She pulled her knees and shoes
closer to her body, and held her breath. Principal Hame stormed
into the room and shouted, "I know you're in here. I heard this
door close." His portly chest heaved in and out from excitement.
Even his red face had a slight sheen of sweat. Principal Hame, or
Ham, as the students called him, really did in real life resemble
the pigs he collected. He had an office full of them. And sure
enough, like a pig can sniff out a truffle, this one had found her.

181

Mina tried to rack her brain to think of an excuse as she slowly began to inch out of her hiding spot, but a familiar voice saved her.

"I heard it, too, but I think it was that door," Mrs. Colbert's voice rang out. "In fact, I'm almost positive it was from the south hallway."

Principal Hame grumbled something and stopped right in front of the filing cabinet. He was two feet from discovering her.

"I don't know. I'm sure it was this one."

Constance's voice became silky smooth as her skin took on a translucent glow. "I'm sure you are right. The culprit ducked into a classroom and is probably cowering in fear behind that filing cabinet right there. Or the culprit is probably heading for the nearest school exit. Think about it. It's the trophy case. Who would destroy that? My guess is someone from Barlow High School."

"You are absolutely right." He clapped his hands together and turned on his heel. "Barlow High has always been trying to steal our thunder. I bet you they're not done yet. Quick, send security out, comb the halls, the parking lot." His voice drifted off as they exited the classroom and the door clicked softly behind them.

Mina didn't breathe or move till she counted to one hundred. She kept her head down and stayed near the ground as she pulled out the phoenix feather, which was still burning slowly. Its miniscule flames danced around the quill.

Fable

"I believe you gave this to me to help me. So if you want to help me, then help me," she whispered to the feather.

The feather continued to burn brightly, and she studied it closely. Acting on intuition, she leaned forward and began to blow on the feather, right near the flames, the same way she would if she was starting a fire. This time, the flames grew brighter and brighter. She tried to hold onto the feather but dropped it when the light became too much. She could hear the fire crackling, and it grew larger and more out of control.

"What have I done?" Mina panicked and ran to the door, and grabbed the fire extinguisher from the wall. She had never before used one of these and tried to maneuver the hose in the right direction. The fire was burning so hot it turned blue. A scream erupted from the middle of the inferno, and a loud explosion rocked the room. Mina fell backward from the blast and covered her ears. She was going to be caught now. There was no mistaking where that noise had come from.

Mina looked toward where the feather was and saw that the explosion had destroyed two lab stations and transformed them into a pile of ash and rubble. But from the ash another ember continued to burn, and a phoenix began to arise from the rubble.

The phoenix craned its neck and flexed its wings experimentally before turning its black beady eyes in Mina's direction.

"Um, was that supposed to do that?" she asked. The bird just continued to stare. "Okay, I don't know why you gave me that feather, but I think you want to help me, so can you help me? I need to get over to the Fae plane."

A voice invaded her mind—not just any voice, but Nan's. *You are a Grimm. You don't need me to cross over,* the bird said.

"How are you doing that? You sound like Nan," Mina asked, stunned.

The bird shook her head at Mina again, ignoring the question.

"Fine, I know that I'm a Grimm and I should be able to cross over, but I don't know how to yet. I can't do it on command."

This time the voice changed, and it started out as Ever's voice before morphing into Jared's. *Then you need to pass through the gatekeeper.*

"What's a gatekeeper?"

Brody's voice filled her mind. *I'm the gatekeeper.* The phoenix continued to speak to her using the voices of those closest to her.

"So you knew I needed to go to the Fae plane. That's why you wanted to help me."

Yes, help you—help me. Mrs. Wong's Chinese dialect came out. *The Stiltskin has me imprisoned and uses my gifts terribly. I want to make my own deal with you. I'm much more valuable than your brother. Choose me instead,* Sara's voice cried out to her, filled with despair.

"I can't. I have to save my brother."

The phoenix's feathers began to dim a little bit in sadness.

Fable

"But I will find a way to free you. If not today, then soon," Mina promised.

Then I will grant you your wish. I will send you to the Fae plane. The phoenix flew into the air, his feathers burning so bright they were blinding. Mina heard the classroom door open, and Jared rushed into the room in a panic. He saw the bird and began to maneuver around the lab tables. Mina was absorbed with the firebird flying in circles above her, weaving a blazing trail of fire.

"No, Mina, don't!" Jared yelled. "It's too dangerous."

A yellow flash whisked past her shoulder, and the piercing screech ripped through the air again. A vortex of fire whirled above her and began to descend upon her, as if to swallow her whole.

She saw Jared try to grab her arm, but he was fighting the vortex of wind and kept being pushed just out of reach. Her hair whipped around her face painfully and she tried to warn Jared to stay back, but he kept pressing forward.

"I won't let you go."

"I have to go, Jared." She saw his face fill with despair as he realized he couldn't save her, as the fiery vortex swept her up and she disappeared.

Nineteen

Pain! A burning sensation ripped through her. She gasped for air, but nothing but heat filled her lungs. It was as if she was underwater, and when she opened her mouth, something else rushed in instead of oxygen. She panicked and tried to scream, but again nothing would come out. Tears streaked down her cheeks as she thought she was suffocating, slowly dying.

Something punched her in the stomach, and all of a sudden she could breathe again. Winded, she lay immobile until the blinding lights disappeared from her vision.

Mina lifted her head from the grass she was lying in to take in her unfamiliar surroundings. Gone were the brick walls, windows, and desks of the school. Instead, she was surrounded by odd-looking trees and plants and flowers. They were twisted, warped and menacing-looking, and not a single breed was familiar. A few minutes ago it had been daytime, but here it was night.

Fable

"Jared!" Mina called out, and looked around to see if he had made it through the portal. He hadn't. She was alone.

The forest unnaturally echoed her call, and she decided it would be better if she didn't do that again. Who knows what was out in the Fae woods? Gathering her nerve, she stood up and dusted off her pants, and saw the phoenix feather lying on the ground next to her.

But she felt like she had forgotten something. Her hands went to her jacket pocket where she kept the Grimoire, and the pocket was empty. After a few minutes of searching the immediate area, she came to the conclusion that the Grimoire couldn't exist on the same plane as the Fae book. Or it was because it was so tied to Jared that if he didn't cross over to the Fae plane, neither did the book. Either way, she was up a creek, without help.

Instead of standing still, waiting for Stiltskin to find her, she thought she needed to start looking for him or the palace. She started walking and kept getting distracted as some new species or flower caught her eye. Mina stopped and sniffed a flower, and it smelled like...blueberry pie, but better. Curious, she walked over to another bright orange flower and took a careful sniff. It smelled like a mix between snicker doodles and butter pecans.

Even the insects that buzzed around the flowers were larger than any she had ever seen in her own world. There was a yellow bumblebee the size of her fist. She watched as the bee came to land on a large lily, but no sooner had the bee landed than the flower closed up and ensnared the bee. Mina swallowed nervously and decided to give all flowers a very wide berth. Jared was right—even though his world was beautiful, it was also dangerous.

Mina walked along a path until she came to a fork in the road.

"Now where?" she groaned, and accidentally bumped into the branches of a nearby bush. Small lights the size of fireflies lifted off the small berry bush and began to dance around her head.

Captivated, Mina reached out to try to touch one of the lights. One of them flew closer and almost alighted on her finger before flitting away just out of reach. She smiled and kept walking until she heard the most wonderful voice. Melodic, wistful, full of longing. The worry she had felt moments ago was forgotten as the desire to follow the song and dancing lights grew.

Her feet moved on their own accord, and she followed the song away from the fork in the road, onto a different, almost indiscernible path that led deeper into the woods and toward a large lake.

Mina was enthralled. Never before had she seen or heard something so glorious, so enchanting, so unnatural, and something told her she needed to possess it—if only it would stop moving over the lake. The song grew louder when Mina paused and hesitated, urging her on.

Fable

Her sneaker dipped into the water's edge, and she lingered momentarily as the cold seeped through the canvas, but it wasn't enough. Shaking off any hesitation, she listened to the song and stepped farther into the water. She could always dry her shoes later, but right now, right this moment, she needed to obey the song more than she needed anything else, and nothing was going to stop her.

A few steps later, the water was up to her knees, but she was undeterred and waded farther into the stream. She could swim; she wasn't afraid. Moments later the water was up to her waist, and a triumphant smile reached her lips. The smile only lasted for a second, replaced by fear as something large grabbed her around the legs and pulled her under the water.

She didn't have time to scream as an icy chill wrapped around her and she plunged deep into the dark water. The dancing lights fading from above the water no longer seemed so beautiful. Now they seemed deadly as they illuminated her watery grave.

Mina tried to struggle and kick at the thing that grasped her foot, but it held her like a vise. A momentary illumination from the light gave Mina a glimpse of what had captured her, and the image terrified her to the core.

It was a young woman. Her skin shimmered like scales, and her long hair, the color of seaweed, flowed past her waist. But her huge cat-like eyes were black as night, and they glared hungrily at her.

Mina's mouth opened to scream in terror. Water rushed past her lips, and she unconsciously swallowed. She panicked and tried to swim up to the surface, but the sea witch clung on and pulled her lower. Mina could feel herself starting to black out, and unlike moments ago when her mind was muddled with an enchantment, now she had control of her full faculties, and she did the only thing she could do. She let the cold seep into her bones until she felt the familiar tingle of power. It could have been her body shutting down and losing feeling in her fingers, but she didn't think so. She didn't have much time.

She reached into her jeans pocket, which was a struggle in itself, and pulled out the shard of glass and held it in the sleeve of her jacket. She swung the shard of glass downward and missed the monster. She tried again and again, and on the third try, she stabbed the water witch in the hand.

The witch ceased in her struggle to overpower Mina. She became paralyzed and released her hold on her. Mina watched as her attacker sank into the darkness below, her body slowly turning to gold as if Stiltskin himself had touched her. The witch sank with her hand outstretched, her last moment of humanity slowly slipping away. Instinctively, Mina tried to grab the woman's hand and swim upward with her, but she couldn't. The witch was dead weight and pulling her down farther. Left with no choice, Mina had to let go of the witch's hand, and she watched as she slowly disappeared into the darkness below, a golden carcass.

Fable

Remembering her predicament, she tried to swim toward the surface, but it was too far, and she was so tired. She shouldn't have wasted those precious seconds trying to save the monster that was trying to kill her. Now she was going to die anyway. Her eyes started to close, and she saw something green rocket through the water in her direction. She had just enough time to realize it was another monster...and it had come to finish her off.

Twenty

Her mouth was dry and her eyes were crusted shut. Her hands felt like giant hammers pummeling her face as she tried to wipe away the offending crud to open them. Something hard and cool was pressed against her mouth, and she pinched them shut against the unknown liquid being forced down her lips. She heard a sigh of frustration before green fingers appeared over her nose and gave a slight pinch.

Mina gasped in alarm, and her mouth opened. The cup was back at her mouth, and she felt something cool and minty fill her mouth. *Don't swallow. Don't swallow,* she told herself, and when the cup moved away, she turned her head and spat out the liquid. She tried to knock the helping green hands away, but her own body had trouble obeying her commands. The green hand came to her mouth again, and she used every bit of effort to bite at the offending fingers.

"Hey. Ouch!" a male voice grumbled.

Fable

Mina turned her muddled head to stare at the green-skinned young man. His green hair was medium length, just touching the edge of his neck, and flowed back and forth as if it was being tossed in an invisible current. He was lean and well-muscled, like a swimmer. He wasn't wearing a shirt but long green pants that looked to be made of grass or seaweed.

"Wh-who are you?" Her voice was wrecked, and she had to lick her lips and swallow a few times before she sounded normal.

The young man turned, shaking his injured finger in the air, and gave her a wary look before answering, "Nix."

"You saved me, didn't you?" She couldn't tear her eyes away from his skin, which out of the water looked very human, except for the greenish tint. If he moved, the light would catch the faintish shimmer of his scales.

"Yes, I almost couldn't revive you, so I'm sorry if you're a little sore."

Mina was wondering why her chest felt like an elephant had been sitting on it.

"Thank you…Nix, is it? What an odd name."

"It's a perfectly good name for a nixie." He looked offended and held out his bitten hand, and small translucent webbing appeared between each of his fingers. When he was positive they were all intact, they disappeared again.

Whoa! she thought. So this is what a nixie looked like.

Nix looked at her again, and this time stood up and moved even farther away from her, then sat closer to a water-filled hole in the ground. He sat on the edge and put both of his feet into the water, and stared at her from a distance.

Mina sat up, and one hand went to her rib cage in pain. She must have been passed out for a while, because all of her clothes were dry. She looked around at her prison. She was in a cave, and the walls were covered with glowing crystals that created the luminescent light. There was a small bed, which she was lying in, a blanket, a cup, and a small pack of items by a far wall, but no obvious exit.

"What did you do to her?" he asked warily.

"You mean the girl who tried to kill me?" Mina answered.

He nodded.

"I'm not sure. I stabbed her with a piece of golden glass, and she changed," Mina replied, trying to sound nonchalant.

He looked at her, and she felt herself shiver under his dark stare. And then she realized the difference between Nix and the woman. Where the sea witch's eyes were an intense black, Nix's cat-shaped eyes were bright green and still very human-looking.

"You're different. You and her." Mina pointed to his eyes. "Her eyes were filled with evil."

Nix's green skin turned an odd shade as he paled and refused to meet her gaze. He leaned forward and ran his fingers through the water as if he took comfort from its touch.

"Yes. She was seduced by our own blood." He sighed and pulled his leg from the water, and leaned his chin on his knee. "Water witch, sea witch, nixies…we are all one and the same.

194

Fable

Cursed by our own desires, so most think of us as evil. But I tell you, we are not born that way. We are gentle creatures. Once we reach a certain age, our power over water fades and we become desperate, thirsty for that power again. And then we have to make a choice: to eventually lose our connection with water, grow old, and die, or begin drowning and killing innocents to feed on and live forever."

Fear raked through her body. Her eyes searched the cave again, looking for another way out, until it dawned on her. The water-filled hole. The only way out was through the water, and Nix was blocking the way.

Nix could see her fear and raised his voice. "Yes, but not all of us are like that! Look at me! Look at my eyes. I'm not like her. I've not become seduced by lust for power. Raina wasn't always like that, either." Nix looked so heartbroken and alone that she couldn't help but feel sorry for him.

"What happened between you?"

"We were in love once. We made a promise to each other to grow old and die together. To not give in to the curse of our race. We thought we were stronger than the temptation, which usually surfaces once we reach adulthood. But then one day last year, I found her crying in the shallows of the water. She could no longer hear the fishes' thoughts, or speak to the tadpoles. No matter how much she sang to them, they never answered. I told her it was okay, she could still speak to me. She was older than I am, so it affected her first. It's scary, to see a curse affect

195

someone you love and knowing that it would be my fate as well."

"Yes, it is," Mina said, thinking of her own troubles.

Nix nodded; he was lost deep in thought. She thought he was done, but he turned his head, and she could see that there was a tear sliding down his delicately scaled cheek.

"I told her we would suffer together, that I would always be there for her until our very end. Then I awoke one morning to a song—her song, and I knew. I knew she had made her choice, and I didn't stop her. I could have. I knew what she was doing, but I refused to watch. I was scared. I was scared that I would join her and turn, too." He sniffed and then looked up proudly into Mina's eyes. His deep green eyes filled with tears. "But I haven't."

Mina couldn't help but feel sorry for Nix and Raina's lost love, and wiped at the corner of her eye as a tear began to manifest.

"She is no longer the Raina I knew and loved. She is a monster, a true sea witch, and I am cursed to die alone."

"And I'm cursed to die during a fairy tale, so we won't go out alone." Mina laughed softly.

Nix leapt up from the water's edge and stumbled away from her. "You're a Grimm! Here on the Fae plane."

"Yes, and you're a nixie. So what?"

Fable

"But—but there are too many tales involving us and Grimms, and we are the ones who end up dead. I don't want to be a part of that."

Mina sighed loudly. "I think it's already too late. If you didn't want to get involved, you should have let me drown."

He stood there, silent, before he nodded in agreement. "Yes. You're right. I should have let you drown." He dove into the water, and like a fish shot through the murky depths and disappeared. Mina went to the water's edge and looked into the darkness, and knew that he'd abandoned her to die.

Twenty~One

Mina picked up the cup that Nix had been trying to coerce her to drink from and dropped it into the watery abyss, counting how many seconds it took before she could no longer see it. It disappeared into the blackness after three. Who knew if there even was a bottom? She sat back on her heels and tried to not panic. They were probably in an underwater cavern that was only accessible from, well, under the water. But what if there was a maze of caverns. If she could hold her breath long enough, she might be able explore or find a way out. Or she might drown in her attempts.

What to do? She chewed on her bottom lip as she looked around the small cave and contemplated her options. This was not the time to break down and cry. This was the time to be smart. Mina went to Nix's pack and dug through the items he had left behind. He had a few small sacks with shells in them, some twine, a knife, and a lidded jar with some blue liquid in it.

Fable

A plan began to form in her mind, and she took the knife, went to the cavern wall, and began to dig out one of the glowing stones. Again and again she scraped, hit, and pried at only the red and green stones, being careful to separate them into two piles.

When she had what she thought was a sufficient amount, she dumped out the bag filled with shells and replaced them with the stones. She washed out the jar, phoenix feather inside it, resealing it with the wax and twine. When fully dry and protected from the water, the feather created a warm glowing light inside the jar. She had gotten the idea from Jared's Coke bottle. When the feather became wet, the fiery light burned down to almost nothing until it was fully dry again.

Mina then went to work on making a weapon out of the shard of the Stiltskin's glass. She found a piece of wood and attached the glass shard to it by wrapping it with more twine, creating a small knife. She made a sheath out of seaweed, and attached the knife and sheath to her thigh with twine. Mina was pretty proud of her ingenuity and was ready to test out her plan.

She took off her shoes and jacket. After tying her hair back with a piece of string she found and using more of the string, she attached the two sacks and the jar with the phoenix feather to her shorts. She then took her first plunge and gasped at how cold the water was against her skin. The water could only be this cold if the cavern was really deep. Mina took a couple of dunks and started to practice deep breathing and counting how long she could hold her breath. She refused to die in an underground cave on the Fae plane alone. She had to save her brother.

Confident that she could hold her breath for at least a minute, she took one last look around the cave before taking a breath and beginning her escape. It was dark, and the jar with the feather created a beautiful warm glow against the shadows. She could see at least two paths, and who knew how many more after that. She was going to have to leave a breadcrumb trail back to this cave if she got lost.

Mina dropped the first glowing green stone under the opening to the cave and was surprised that there was an actual bottom. It stopped there and continued to glow. She swam a few yards down the tunnel to her left and dropped another green stone. She swam a few more yards before deciding to retrace her path back up into the cavern again for another breath. This was going to take awhile, and she was tiring quickly. Mina repeated the actions, breathing, following the same tunnel until it came to a dead end, and then replacing the green stones with red ones to mark the lack of exits.

She had started down the right tunnel, following her same pattern of dropping green stones, when she found another hole in the ceiling of the tunnel. Could it be an exit? Could it be another cavern with air? She kicked her legs and swam hard for the opening, and broke the surface with a huge gasp. There was air. Yes!

Fable

But this cavern was the same as the other, filled with glowing stones and completely empty. She didn't want to spend too much time dawdling, so she took another breath and kept swimming. She swam to another fork in the tunnels and another dead end. Mina needed air and more stones, so she retreated to the second cavern and refilled her bag of red and green stones. She could do this, she thought to herself. If there were caverns with air all around down here, she might just make it out…alive.

Mina was on her fourth tunnel when she began to start feeling lightheaded and dizzy. This was becoming too much for her. She was about to swim back to another cavern air pocket when she saw a bigger opening and more light coming from above. Was it a way out? She pushed off the ground and swam hard for the beacon of light above her. It looked different, so she prayed for it to be an exit.

Her head broke through the water, and she felt a cool breeze against her face. She smiled in relief. Treading water, she wiped her eyes, only to see that she hadn't exactly escaped. It was just another larger cavern filled with even more glowing stones. Her heart plummeted. She was still trapped.

Something moved in the corner, and Mina's intrusion startled it. At first she thought it was a snake, or a pile of leaves because of the way it rustled and moved, but a head slowly raised itself off the floor and turned to look at her. There was no mistaking the black cat-like eyes of a sea witch. It hissed at her and began to crawl across the floor in her direction. Mina screamed in fright and dove under the water to try to swim away from it.

It was a terrible choice. She didn't get a great breath, and her fear and adrenaline were making her escape clumsy. Mina took off down a tunnel that she hadn't marked with stones. She looked back behind her and saw something green plummet through the water on her tail. It was fast—faster than she could swim. She knew it. There was no way she could out-swim it; she was going to have to fight it.

She turned and pulled out the knife off her thigh and waited for the witch to come to her. The witch's black eyes filled her with terror, but Mina held the blade in front of her and continued to tread water. The monster barreled straight at her, its long claw-like hands reaching for her, when something shot out of the darkness and smashed the witch into the wall.

Mina had never heard a scream like the one she heard under the water. It was awful as the two beings fought against each other. It was Nix. He was smashing the witch against a cavern wall, using his full weight to keep her pinned. He was physically bigger than the sea witch, but it was obvious that since he didn't feed on innocents, he wasn't as strong as she was.

His voice pounded into her head. *The tunnel to the left. Hurry.*

She grasped her head in pain, but she didn't waste the time Nix was buying her. Mina swam as hard as she could to the tunnel, and, sure enough, she could see it: the exit. It was an opening twenty feet across and ten feet high. But it seemed so far away. Her lungs burned for air, but she focused on her goal and kept swimming. Her legs felt like lead weights and her arms like Jell-o. But she continued swimming until she passed through the opening and headed upward. She could see it. The sky. It danced across the water through a sea of glass. Her heart sank when she realized it was farther than she could hold her breath. Even now, bubbles were escaping from her lips, and she was out of strength.

Her body's lack of oxygen was causing her to hallucinate, and all of a sudden she could see Brody's smiling face floating in front of her. She reached out to touch it, and it disappeared, to be replaced by Jared's angry one, yelling at her.

Swim, Mina! Fight—don't give up!

"I'm tired, Jared. I can't. I'm so tired," she mentally called back before her body betrayed her and her muscles cramped underwater, and she felt herself sinking lower and lower.

NOO! She heard a scream and was unsure if it was her own hallucination of Jared or someone else. Something hard and rough grabbed her around the waist, and she was being propelled through the water faster than she had ever gone in her life, straight for the light. But Mina knew she wouldn't make it. Her body went limp, and her eyes had closed on their own when something warm pressed against her lips.

She didn't have the energy to fight, and was surprised when her mouth was forced open and life-saving oxygen passed into her mouth. She opened her eyes in surprise to find Nix's lips pressed to hers, kissing her. No, breathing for her as he continued to swim upward. Her hands reached up to grab his face and hold it to her mouth hungrily as if her life depended on his kiss—which it did. His kiss fought off the darkness of death, and her mind began to function again. She was kissing a monster!

A few seconds later they broke through the water, and she pulled away from his lips to breathe on her own. Nix carefully held her and swam toward shore. Mina only had the strength to roll over on her back and let him pull her to safety. He had now saved her life three times.

Rocks brushed against her feet and she tried to stand up, only to fall to her knees in the rocky shallows. Nix held onto her arm and tried to support her weight. He desperately pulled her away from the water, and even though they were on the shore, he didn't stop. He tried to coerce her to move, but she couldn't. Mina collapsed on the ground.

She felt warm arms wrap around her, and then she was being lifted through the air. Nix had picked her up and continued to run away from the lake as far as he could. A short time later, he found a small clearing in which to stop, and he gently put her down. He was out of breath and collapsed on the ground, watching the path behind them, looking for a pursuer.

Mina rolled on the ground, her body shaking from the cold and the near asphyxiation, and stared at Nix's muscled green back in utter confusion. She thought he had abandoned her to

Fable

die, that he didn't want anything to do with her or the Grimm curse. If so, why did he save her...again? But her thoughts continued to dance as she felt herself slipping into an exhausted sleep.

Mina awoke with a start and listened carefully to the sound of footsteps treading quietly past her. She tried to move her arm, but it was numb from her sleeping on it awkwardly. Instead, she played opossum and watched through lowered lashes as the sound came again and a shadow passed by her. Her heart skipped a beat when her vision was filled with a green silhouette. She immediately thought the sea witch had found her, but then she sighed when she realized that it was just Nix. He had found a stick and climbed one of the odd twisted trees.

His tall, nimble green body slithered up the tree, proving that he was just as agile on land as he was in water. Nix swung the stick with ease at the nearest branch, and two pieces of fruit fell to the ground and rolled along the grass. He dropped the stick and began his descent.

Mina touched her fingers to her lips as the memory of his life-saving kiss came flooding back to her. She was grateful that he couldn't see her cheeks burning in embarrassment. Deciding that the immediate threat was over, she slowly sat up and stretched. Her whole body ached from head to toe, and she couldn't help but feel like a ton of bricks had landed on her chest. Nix came over and handed a small piece of fruit to her. It was only slightly bruised from the fall.

"Here, eat this," he commanded, before moving to sit across from her. His skin looked lighter under the morning sun, less green.

"I don't think I'm supposed to eat the food in the Fae world," she said.

"That's true for most food here. It can be addicting to your kind, but as far as aftereffects go, this is the mildest fruit there is."

Mina took the odd-looking purple fruit and sniffed it carefully before rolling it between her fingers. She was starving, but even the simplest temptation could endanger her whole reason for being here.

"What happened back there?" she asked, hoping he would know she was referring to the sea witch. "And why did you save me, when I thought you were leaving me to die?"

Nix looked at her carefully over his own piece of fruit before raising the fruit in the air like a toast and taking his own careful bite. "You had an unfortunate run-in with one of the oldest and strongest sea witches around...my mother."

"Your mother? I thought that...well, I don't know what I thought. I just figured that you and Raina were the only ones left."

"We are, I mean...were, the only *nixies* left. The rest have all changed. So I try to stay out of their waterways as much as possible. But you, you trespassed right into her home. You're lucky I came when I did, or you'd be dinner. But I've got to hand it to you. You're either crazy stupid or crazy brave for what you attempted. You'd almost made it out."

"It doesn't matter. I was crazy either way, but I wouldn't have done it if I didn't think I was going to die in that cave. You could have told me you were going to come back." Mina paused in thought and then said in a softer, uncertain voice, "You were going to come back, right?"

His shoulders dropped, and Nix looked at the ground. "I needed time to think, to decide what I was going to do with my life. You killed the one person I loved."

"But she was a monster. You said so yourself."

"Yes, and I know no one has ever come back once turned. But after running into you, I knew that I would be pulled into whatever quest you're currently embarking on. I, too, know of the book and the deal made with the Grimms. I also know of how the stories end for most of the nixies. Not good. So I had to decide if I was going to purposely turn, or join you on your quest and die sooner rather than later."

Mina's fingers dug into the purple fruit, and she stared at him in disbelief. "So you left because you couldn't decide if you were going to kill me and join the monsters or help me. Talk about peer pressure," she replied sarcastically. "So much for going out all noble."

Nix stood up and began to pace back and forth. "No, you see, that's what I thought at first. I thought living near Raina, even though she was a monster, would be enough for me, but now that she's dead, I thought I should be the one to take revenge for her death, but I can't. I told you before that we are gentle creatures until we turn. So I decided that if I can't live with Raina, I don't want to live without her."

He stopped pacing and sat on the ground, eye to eye with Mina. His hands crumpled into tight fists. Mina could tell this was a difficult conversation for him.

His bright green eyes looked deeply into hers, pleading with her to understand. "I turned seventeen last month, and, like Raina did, I've lost my ability to hear the creatures of the water. And I can no longer control the currents. I can feel myself getting older, becoming weaker. It won't be long now…I'm dying, Mina. "

Mina stared at the passionate Nix with utter shock. She could tell from the way he spoke that he was serious.

He swallowed cautiously and didn't stutter one word when he valiantly said, "I would rather die now helping you in whatever quest you're on than to live as a monster without her.

She repeated his own words back to him. "You're either crazy stupid, or crazy brave."

"Either way, I'm just crazy." He chuckled softly.

"Well, crazy always likes company. So, do you think you're up for a dangerous quest that will probably get us both killed?"

Fable

Nix got up, only to kneel before Mina. His green hair still mysteriously swayed, but now that they were farther away from the water, it moved less. His piercing green eyes were filled with determination as he grasped her hand and muttered, "I don't fear death—death should fear me."

Twenty~Two

Mina couldn't believe her luck. After she told Nix her story and about her quest to save her brother Charlie, he was actually even more gung-ho to help her. Probably because it was a life-saving mission. What was even more unbelievable was that Nix knew how to get to the Fates' palace. It seemed too easy, too simple. So she knew better than to take it for granted. But first they had to make it to the palace, which, according to Nix was at least two days' journey on foot.

"I really wish we had a faster mode of transportation," Mina said, after she tripped over another tree root and fell face down in a pile of leaves. That was the third time she'd tripped in the last two hours.

"What's a mode of transportation?" Nix asked, and helped her back up.

Fable

"Um, an automobile, a car...you know, *vroom vroom*." She made a driving and sitting motion. Goodness, she sounded stupid.

Nix just looked at her in confusion, and then his face brightened. "Oh, I get it. This way." He motioned for her to follow him, and he walked back toward the river they had very carefully been skirting. They'd been careful to follow it so they wouldn't lose their way, but he always carefully kept a wary distance. He paused at the river and hesitated.

"What's the matter?" she asked.

"I don't know if they'll answer me. I haven't been able to talk with them. They may not even come, so don't get your hopes up." He walked along the riverbed amongst the tall grass until he found a blue speckled reed. Using a sharp rock, he quickly carved out three holes and another toward the top.

Mina watched in fascination, and once his whistle was done, Nix waded out to the middle of the river and began to play a silent song. His hair began to come to life again and flow widely with the rushing water. His mouth blew, his fingers moved, but Mina didn't hear a single note from the flute. On and on he played his silent flute, but nothing happened. After two more songs, he walked out of the river and sat on the bank solemnly.

"I couldn't hear anything," Mina said.

"That's because you're human. You can't hear the beautiful music I played for them. It would have paid for our passage, but

I don't know. I couldn't hear the music, either. I had to play from memory." He flopped onto his back and stared at the sky.

"They've never before taken so long to come. I'm sorry. I failed you," Nix groaned.

"Who, Nix? Who were you trying to call?"

"The kelpies. But I should have known it wouldn't work." He ran his hands through his hair in frustration and let out a really long sigh. "I haven't been able to hear them in a while."

Mina knew he was thinking about the consequences of staying a nixie, and everything he had lost.

"It's fine, really. I don't mind the walking."

"No, it's not fine. I think we're being followed, and I can't stray too far from water without weakening further. We need the kelpies if we want to outrun her."

"Who…you mean the sea witch is still after us?" Mina asked, balking.

"Yes, it's because I helped you escape. She's tracking us. I keep crossing the streams, following along different paths, but she knows and I know that I can't stray far from a water source."

"Why is she so set on getting us?"

"It's because I interfered. This isn't just any sea witch following us…it's my mother, and she won't stop until she's found us." Frustrated, he lunged up from his sitting position and hurled the reed flute into the middle of the river. It made a plunking sound, then disappeared. Nix had turned and begun to walk up the riverbank toward Mina when a loud rushing sound caught their attention. He turned back to the river; a wide smile formed across his face.

"They came," he said in awe, as if he hadn't really believed they would come.

Mina turned to watch the middle of the river become a vortex of swirling, rushing water. The waves collided against each other, and the noise was loud, like a crashing waterfall. An otherworldly sound erupted from the middle of the river, and a glorious translucent head came from the center of the vortex. It was a horse made of water. Then another one stepped from the middle of the river, and then another. Six beautiful translucent beasts stood before them, shimmering and reflecting back Mina's and Nix's own images.

The horses walked toward them but stopped at the water's edge. The lead horse separated from his brethren, and as soon as he touched his hoof to the rocky shore, he transformed like a snake shedding his skin. The lead horse's coat turned white, while the others stayed in their translucent Fae form, safe in the water's embrace.

Nix ran to the horse and pressed his face to its muzzle. The white horse pressed against him in mutual delight. A second or two later, Nix pulled away with a frown on his face. "Oh, how I wish I could hear your sweet voice again."

"Will they take us?" Mina asked. She was somewhat hopeful and scared of riding the beast at the same time.

"I can only ask." Nix leaned forward and began to speak with the kelpie, but all Mina heard was a soft clicking and popping nose, similar to how a dolphin would speak.

She watched closely for the kelpie's reaction. The lead horse walked back to the others, and they started to step back into the middle of the river.

"What's going on? Are they leaving?" she asked fearfully.

"I don't know," Nix said slowly.

The white horse was still in a physical form, and there seemed to be a bit of a discussion going on between them. One of the horses neighed and rose up on his hind legs, his front hooves kicking the air in displeasure. Others danced about sideways, while some shook their manes.

"Oh, geez, Nix, you didn't tell them I was a Grimm, did you? Probably not the surest way to gain their trust or help," Mina said sarcastically.

His face turned a weird shade of brown. "Uh, I might have mentioned it."

Mina rolled her eyes and continued to watch one of the most beautiful scenes she had ever seen. One horse, then two, turned and disappeared into the river's waves. Then a third left, followed by a fourth. They were leaving. Only one kelpie remained with the white one. It was a smaller horse by a few hands and it still looked young, but it followed the white horse bravely to where they stood. When the little horse reached the embankment and stepped out, his watery coat turned a dark red.

214

Fable

Mina stood and stared at his coat. This wasn't a shade of red that had ever appeared on a horse; it was blood red. She had to wonder if the other kelpies had actually stepped out of the water, what color their coats would have been. This was the Fae plane. Nothing came in average packaging.

Both horses came and stood in front of them. The white one leaned down, and Nix nimbly leapt upon his back. The red one followed suit, and Mina did her best to not embarrass herself as she fumbled onto the kelpie's back.

The horses turned and began to run alongside the river. Mina couldn't help but feel the excitement of riding a mythical creature in a foreign land and grin. She laughed out loud and wrapped her fingers around the red kelpie's mane. Nix looked over his shoulder and laughed with her at their exhilarating ride. They ran unbelievably fast. The trees, boulders, and forest whisked by, and with every step the kelpies took, a clear wet hoof print was left behind.

She reached down and patted the horse's neck, and whispered, "You're magnificent." She wasn't positive, but it seemed like the horse shook his head at her and proceeded to show her how magnificent he was by racing ahead faster, catching up to Nix's horse and then passing him at a river bend. Mina couldn't help but turn around and blow a playful kiss at Nix as they sped past him. His face showed complete shock, but he leaned forward and whispered to his horse, and then the race was on.

The kelpies raced neck and neck through the woods. They were as playful on land as they were in the water, taking turns, letting one horse run ahead, then running up a separate pass to jump in front of them in surprise. When Mina was once again in the lead, they ran too close to the riverbed, and a huge wave erupted out of the river to dump right on her head.

"EEEEEEK!" Mina shrieked as Nix ran past again. "That's not fair!" she called after him. Red, for she had no other name to call him by, took off like a cat after a mouse and did something completely uncalled for. He jumped into the river and disappeared beneath her, forming into water again. Mina flailed in the water, thinking the horse was completely gone, but then she could feel him, like a giant current that had her in the palm of his hand, and they were speeding along the river at breakneck speeds, even passing Nix and the white horse.

It was the oddest and scariest thing she had ever done, to whiz down a river at such speeds. She thought she was going to smash onto a large rock, but the current of water that was the kelpie moved her out of the way. When they were ahead of Nix, the current picked up Mina and literally threw her out of the river toward the rocky embankment. Mina screamed and flung her arms out in front of herself to try to break her fall, but at the last minute, the wave flowed after her and then under her. Reappearing as the red kelpie, the horse made a watery snicker and kicked up its heels at the horse behind them.

Fable

She clutched his mane and cried out loudly, "Please don't do that again. Or at least give a little warning next time." She wasn't sure, but she thought he bobbed his head in agreement.

The horses calmed down their crazy Kentucky Derby after Red was the obvious winner, and then they slowed to a peaceful pace.

"So tell me about yourself," Nix said.

"What? Now?"

"Yes, I want to know what it's like to be human, and why you would sacrifice everything to save your brother."

Mina thought for a minute and then began to tell him about her life. How they always moved from state to state until the curse found them. She told him of how her friends would sometimes get wrapped up in the tales as well. When he became increasingly interested, she decided to tell him a little about each of her friends.

"Who's Nan?" he asked when she described the Snow White quest.

"Well, Nan has been my best friend ever since I moved to Kennedy High School. She kind of took me under her wing and refused to let me become the obvious wallflower. She adored my brother Charlie, is a huge reality TV fan, and loves…loves her cell phone."

Nix's face took on another odd expression, and she realized that he didn't know half of what she was talking about. He probably didn't know what a high school was, or a TV, or a cell phone. It was so easy to just assume that since Jared and Ever knew, that all of the Fae on this world also knew.

"Brody is—" She sighed and felt herself get a little dreamy. "Brody is the most handsome, most popular guy I know, and he also happens to be really sweet. He plays on the water polo team at school, and I think you would like it. It's a game with a ball and net played in a swimming pool."

Nix's eyes lit up at the mention of water polo. He made Mina spend the next half hour describing everything about this wonderful game played in the water. Mina was sure that she only knew enough about the sport to fill two minutes, but she found out that she knew more than she thought she did.

"I sure would love to play this water polo here on the Fae plane. Might be a little difficult finding a water creature with the right appendages and limbs to play." Nix then became lost in thought as he obsessed over trying to re-create the game here. "I could make a net out of the forever weed."

"What's forever weed?"

"A weed that lies in the deepest parts of a river. If you wander through it, it wraps around you forever...until you die."

"And you want to make a net out of it? What if someone crashes into it? And it wraps around them and won't let them go?" she blurted, horrified at the thought.

He looked at her as if she was dumb. "Well, any real water creature knows that you just don't crash into it."

Fable

She let him ramble on until the conversation became quiet again.

"I'm sorry, I didn't let you finish," he piped up.

"Finish what?"

"Your story about your friends. Do you have any more? I would like to know more about your life. Raina was my only friend, and now that she's gone, I-I think you are my only friend now."

Mina felt her throat contract with emotion, and she had to force back the tears that threatened to spill forth. What if everyone in her life turned or changed into some kind of a monster and she lost them forever, and she was left alone. Would she be willing to live a life of solitude and die young? Or would she choose the path of darkness? A shiver ran up her spine, and she couldn't help but feel a tingling of apprehension. She had almost given in to the power, and used it once to cause a terrible accident that killed her friend. Until the Fates, or Maeve, the Queen of the Fae, intervened and made a bargain with Mina. Save her son, save her friend. Just one more reminder to never trust the Fae completely.

The horses slowed and came to a halt overlooking a cliff. They were still traveling parallel to the river, which now barreled over the same cliff into what looked like a 300-foot waterfall. It was the first time Mina could actually see the Fae world from a high viewpoint, and what she saw took her breath away. The world was similar to her own human world but completely different. There were two separate suns and three moons, two of which were already making their appearance in the sky. The mix of the suns setting and moons rising created a kaleidoscope of colors painted across the canvas of the sky. If she turned her head, she could see a shooting star trail across the dark blue heavens and disappear into the pink sun. It didn't make sense, it couldn't possibly make sense, but it felt so right.

"It's beautiful," Mina whispered.

"It can be at times," Nix said wearily. "At others times it's too perfect." He waited until the final sun had almost set, and then he pointed in the distance, to what looked like a white snow-capped mountain surrounded by a beautiful crystal lake. "There. That's where we're going."

"I don't see anything." Mina strained and tried to stand taller on the horse to look. She saw a small carriage in the distance, pulled by what looked like a chimera, approach the south side of the lake. The carriage and beast crossed onto a large stone bridge that blended perfectly into the shimmering hues of the lake, unless you were looking for it. She looked ahead to see what was on the other side, but the bridge looked unfinished—like someone had forgotten to complete the north end. The carriage never slowed and didn't seem deterred by the lack of a road. One minute it was there, and the next second the carriage had disappeared into thin air.

"Where did it go?" Mina gasped.

Fable

"Wait for it. Wait for it," Nix chanted, and pointed to the sinking sun and the middle of the lake.

Mina strained her eyes, staring at the spot that Nix had referred to, and then as the sun sank below the horizon, it appeared: the rest of the completed stone bridge that led to a double arched white and gold gate and up to the front steps of a glorious palace. In the moonlight, the walls sparkled and shone, reflecting back the last of the suns' rays.

Her breath caught, and a single tear slid down her cheek at the magnificence of the Fates' home. The north side of the palace nestled into the mountain, protecting it from an invasion. Towers pierced the sky, seeming to disappear among the soft white clouds. Torches inside the castle were lit, and window by window the castle was alight in a soft ethereal glow.

Nix explained that the palace could only be seen at sunset and sunrise, and was hidden the rest of the day. Something flew over the castle, and Mina thought she saw a griffin patrolling the sky. A second one came to land on an outcropping on the mountain and glared watchfully over the lake. Of course the Royal Fates would be protected. She scanned the main entrance into the palace and saw what the veil had hidden. On the other side of the bridge were guards. Not small human guards—the giant variety.

A second later the veil was back up, and the palace disappeared behind its protective glamour once more.

She swallowed nervously. "Now what? How do we get inside with all of the guards?"

"Oh, the giants and the griffins are the least of our worries. We aren't sneaking into the palace by land or air."

"Of course we're not," she replied sarcastically.

"The kelpies once told me of another way in." His smile widened.

"Uh, Nix?" Mina called out worriedly, but it was too late.

Nix smiled. He nudged his horse forward, and it took off running toward the waterfall, then dove off the cliff. Her horse, without prompting, followed the white one and leapt into the air.

Twenty~Three

"Oh, no, no, NO NOOOO!" she screamed as the horse underneath her flew through the air to disappear once again. She felt herself falling, and every inch of her body flailed, trying to stop the terrifying descent. She couldn't catch her breath; she could no longer scream. The jagged rocks at the bottom of the waterfall came rushing toward her, and just when she thought she would be crushed to death, a ball of water appeared around her like a protective bubble and she hit the water hard, but not hard enough to cause any damage.

Inside the bubble, she bounced and moved and was bashed around by the rocks, but nothing could pop the bubble. She was still holding her breath, and a few seconds later they cleared the rocks and dangerous falls. Her bubble appeared above the water, and then a few seconds later the transparent horse was once more securely underneath her. He was swimming quite happily along the stream.

"Holy waterfalls! Let's not do that again…ever!" Mina gushed, holding onto Red for dear life, scared that he would disappear again.

Nix was farther up, and she heard him laugh out loud. Mina looked underneath her and was surprised that the kelpie now resembled a hybrid of a horse and seal. Its long tail was powerful and beat against the river currents rapidly. She was cold and wet, warmed only by the heat from the kelpie itself. She was now extremely grateful that they had traveled by land most of the way. Within minutes they drew closer to where the palace lay hidden.

There was a slight buzzing and *pop!* as they passed through an invisible barrier and the glamour dropped, and there before her was the Fae palace. There wasn't a storybook in all creation that could capture the beauty of the palatial structure. The palace walls shimmered as if they were covered in mystical fairy dust. The arched gate was made of silver and gold, and a sun and moon were prominent in all of the decorations and flags that adorned the castle. Even from a distance she could see the sun and moon shapes embedded into the stone bridge itself. Even the street was made of marble pieces in the shapes of silver moons and golden suns.

Mina's heart began to beat wildly when she saw one of the giants harassing and arguing with the driver of the carriage. Apparently, he was not welcome, and a second later a scream and a *whoosh* was heard as the carriage, driver, and chimera went flying into the air off the bridge and into the water.

Within seconds two pairs of green eyes glowing in the shadows appeared from beneath the bridge and started toward the shocked driver, who was struggling to make it to shore. Nix leaned over and whispered *trolls* to her. Mina didn't need the prompting; she knew exactly what they were. The chimera was able to quickly get out of the water, and flew to the bridge and took off running, but the Fae carriage driver was not so lucky.

The kelpies had stopped around the last little bend of the river before the palace and carefully treaded water, keeping their distance from the trolls and their victim. Within seconds the sound of gasping and splashing water disappeared, followed by a scream. A long minute later, the green eyes popped back up under the shadows of the bridge, signaling the trolls' return. They were now even more watchful.

"What do we do now?" Mina whispered, shivering either from the cold of the water or the fear that penetrated her whole body. "I don't have the Grimoire to help me. I have nothing to capture them in on this plane."

Nix rubbed his hand through the kelpie's mane and studied the layout of the palace. He looked concerned as well, but gazed at her in disbelief.

"Are you kidding? Mina, look at me," he commanded.

Shivering with uncertainty, she looked into Nix's green cat-eyes and saw utter faith.

"You don't need a weapon," he said softly. "You are your greatest weapon."

She closed her eyes and let his confidence and words soak into her very core. He was right. If this Fae believed in her, then she wasn't going to let him down.

"Let's do this before I change my mind," she said firmly. "Now, how do we get in?"

Nix's face lit up with excitement, and he rubbed the back of his neck. "Okay, I've got a plan, but I don't think you're going to like it."

She stared at him through narrowed eyes. "Nix," she said in warning tones.

His cheeks turned that odd brown color again, when he blushed. "Um, it requires us to swim underwater from here under the bridge, past the guards, up to an underwater duct that leads to an indoor waterfall that empties into a bathing chamber."

Mina quickly calculated the distance and knew there was no way she could hold her breath that long. She looked at Nix's blushing face and back at the water, and she knew exactly how he was planning on getting her that far.

"Uh-uh, I would rather go through the front door and tackle the giants than have to life-saving-suck-kiss you for five minutes. How in the world am I going to explain this to…" Her cheeks also turned deep red as she imagined explaining this to Brody. And then she remembered she wasn't dating Brody, and she wasn't even sure how Jared would feel about her kissing someone. He probably wouldn't even care. She thought of Charlie in a fiery prison, and that clinched it.

She wasn't going to let her own modesty and shyness keep her from her goal. She was in another world, playing by different rules, and if she wanted any normal chance at a relationship...with anyone...then she needed to finish these quests. All of them.

Nix wasn't offended in the least by Mina's rejection of him. In fact, he looked a little relieved himself. "Well, I might be able to distract the giants from the gates, and you can run across, but the trolls would be on the bridge in seconds flat."

"Okay, okay. I like your way better. Under the bridge and under the water it is."

He shrugged and wouldn't look her in the eye. "All right, then. Life-saving-suck-kiss it is." He pinched his lips together and quickly turned away, but Mina could see his shoulders rising and falling in rapid succession. He was laughing at her. And then she realized how absurd it sounded and started laughing, too.

Even the kelpies seemed to pick up on their laughter and started to dance in the water. Which drew attention to their area of the lake.

"Uh-oh." Nix calmed down instantly. "They know someone's here." The trolls' green eyes were moving in their direction. And even the giants had moved to stare out across the water.

"We need to move quickly," Mina hissed.

"Yes, it's now or never." Nix slid off the kelpie, and Mina followed suit. He quickly leaned in and pressed his head to the white kelpie, and she knew he was trying to give him instructions. A moment later the red kelpie stepped out of the water in full horse form and began running toward the bridge, then stopped right before it. Rising up on his rear hooves, he was a magnificent creature and the perfect distraction. The white kelpie did the same thing and took off in the water toward the trolls, dancing and frolicking mere feet from them, taunting them mercilessly.

Nix held Mina close in the reeds, hiding until he knew that both the trolls and the giants were distracted.

"You ready?" he asked.

She nodded her head mutely.

"Take a deep breath and hold on to me. If you need oxygen, just tug on my hand. And remember, we can't show ourselves and come up for air until we are safely in the palace. Do you understand?"

"Yes," she whispered.

Nix counted down. "Three—two—one."

And she took a deep breath, and they were under, Mina swimming hand in hand with Nix toward the bridge. He kept trying to pull her deeper toward the bottom of the lakebed so they wouldn't be seen, but every instinct in her body wanted to avoid its murky depths at all costs.

Fable

He motioned with his hands downward, and she finally kicked and followed him down just as a commotion of water flew past them. Mina turned and could see the white kelpie take off toward the reeds, where they had just come from. They were almost to the bridge, and she could look up through the water and barely see one set of green glowing eyes. Had the other troll followed the kelpie? She had hoped for both trolls to follow the horse, but she was still happy if only one did. That meant one fewer monster to try to kill her if they got caught.

She was at her limit and quickly tugged on Nix's arm. He immediately turned and wrapped his arms around her, and pressed his lips to hers.

Sweet air rushed into her mouth, and she let him control the breathing and speed at which they exchanged carbon dioxide and oxygen. It seemed like the polite thing to do. He gently tapped the side of her neck three times, signaling for her to count and start swimming. She immediately understood and took one last breath, and they were off.

He still swam slightly faster than she did, and she probably could have done better if she hadn't started doubting herself all of a sudden. Her plan was stupid, she wasn't strong enough, and even if she got inside, she didn't know how to save her brother. She felt herself slowing down, and Nix continued to pull on her in desperation. He saw that she was freezing up and kept shaking his head at her.

It was no use; the doubt continued to flood her mind like a creepy hypnotizing song. She looked at Nix and shook her head, and pointed up toward the surface. His eyes went wide in horror, and he shook his head.

She couldn't help it. There was no way she could win; she might as well let herself get caught by the trolls. Maybe they would take pity on her and just put her in jail. It was better than death. She was weak—she wasn't brave. She was useless, a poor excuse for a Grimm. The words kept coming, and the song never stopped. If she just let go of Nix's hand, he could escape, and only she would be caught. Yes, yes. That was what she must do.

Mina felt herself let go of Nix's hand, and she kicked toward the surface, toward the green glowing eyes of the troll that was waiting for her under the bridge.

A voice blasted into her consciousness. *DON'T LISTEN!* It was Nix's voice, she could tell, and she could see the struggle it was for him to speak to her. He grasped his head in pain, but then took off after her like a fish through water. He grabbed her bare foot and pulled her down into the water right before she almost broke the surface.

She kicked and struggled against him, but he placed his hands over her ears, and she could see him concentrate.

Don't listen. It's a trap, a siren. They're like a sea witch, but worse. Look at me. I can get you through this. Trust me! He reached forth and pressed his lips to hers, forcing more air into her lungs.

230

Fable

It came as such a relief that she didn't even know she needed air until that moment. The desolate song of fear, doubt, and hopelessness made her completely forget to breathe.

Look there—do you see it?

Mina tried to follow his direction and could see a statue buried deep in the water. It was the statue of a beautiful woman at the bottom of the river, her arms held up in the air as if she was waiting for an embrace from her lover.

That's the siren. Turned to stone by one of the trolls. She is the guardian of the deep water. As long as you can ignore her song, we will make it. He stopped talking into her mind, and she knew that his energy was waning. Nix pulled her, and she kept swimming. They swam right past the stone statue. Mina couldn't tear her eyes away from it.

She wouldn't have made it if it weren't for Nix. She wondered what terrible song the siren had tormented him with; he seemed in pain but otherwise fine. Soon they could no longer feel the siren's touch. Overwhelming feelings continued to plague her, but not so much that she couldn't deal with them.

After two more stops for Nix to help her breathe, they finally made it to an underwater aqueduct. He waved her over and pointed to the small circular entrance that looked barely big enough for her to fit into. She couldn't see inside. It was pitch black. Her hands shook, but she uncovered the jar with the phoenix feather and handed it to Nix. When it was obvious that she wasn't going to enter first, he leaned forward for one more

231

shared breath between them and turned to swim up the tunnel, using the light of the feather to guide him.

Mina pulled a small green stone out of her pouch and followed suit, being careful to stay right on Nix's heels. This tunnel was smaller than the caverns she had previously swum through, and she felt herself become extremely claustrophobic. Nix swam farther, and then turned and swam through a tunnel that went upward. Mina had just braced herself and pushed off after him when something grabbed her foot and pulled her back down.

She fought against whatever was grabbing her and tried to hit it with her fist, but the thing wouldn't let go. The flow from her green stone illuminated the deathly face and familiar black hate-filled eyes of the sea witch.

The hag's face smiled widely to reveal several sharp pointy fangs, and her hand swatted the stone from Mina's grip. She dropped it, and the glow disappeared, leaving her in complete darkness with the monster.

Twenty~Four

Panic overcame Mina as the darkness threatened to swallow her whole. Was this her grim end? She tried to swim away again but felt the witch's hands grasp her legs. Pain laced through her where the crooked claws raked against her skin. But it was that painful slash which reminded her of her own weapon. She reached toward her thigh and pulled out her glass knife, and frantically tried to stab the witch, but she couldn't see her and missed.

A yellow glow filled the small space as Nix reappeared. He looked horrified and rushed in to help Mina. But now there were too many bodies and not enough room to maneuver. Someone or something kicked her hand, and she dropped the knife. She was also out of air and needed to find some...now. She tried to push off and kick up the tunnel again, but the witch grabbed her and pulled her down. Mina tried to push her off but then felt the witch stiffen and freeze. Her snarling face froze in a mask of horror and pain as something stabbed her in the back. The witch's scream died on her lips, and her black cat-eyes clouded over, turning gold.

The witch sank, freeing Mina, and she couldn't help but stare at Nix's horrified face as he held her Stiltskin-empowered knife. He had saved her, but had killed his own mother. He slowly sat down in the tunnel and buried his face in his hands. Mina tried to motion that she needed air, but he wasn't paying attention. He was lost in his own misery. She grabbed his shoulder and shook, but he went limp and stared at the knife in his hands.

Frustrated, she pushed off and swam as hard as she could toward the tunnel that Nix had gone up. This one had to lead out; it was her only chance. She kicked until she felt a sucking current that began to pull her up. She was no longer swimming but being carried forcefully along a pipeline. Her head broke the surface of the water, and she had just enough time to breathe and duck as she was swept into a tunnel and then down a long slope. Faster and faster she traveled until she could see an opening, and then a drop.

Didn't Nix mention something about an indoor waterfall that led to an inner bathing pool? He just didn't say how big it was. Squelching any scream or sound, she tried to hold it together as she was thrown over the drop. This time she was prepared for the fall, and it wasn't more than thirty feet before she plunged into the small pool. She was careful; she kept her head under the water and tried to look up and through the reflection for signs of life. There was a shadow, but then it moved away.

Mina kicked along the bottom of the pool and found a statue of a mermaid on a pedestal pouring water out of a jar. Keeping her head low, she hid behind the water feature and peeked around. Since it was nighttime, there weren't as many Fae around. She saw someone in a robe walk past, and she quietly slid back down into the water and made her plan. The hall was dark; torches lined the walls, casting eerie shadows along the marble floor. Luckily, there were tons of potted plants, statues, and décor for her to hide behind.

First off, she needed to get out of her wet clothes and tend to her leg wound from the sea witch. Second, well, second, she needed to think of a better plan than getting dry clothes. She swam to the edge of the bathing pool, which was barely deep enough for her to stand up in, and crawled over the ledge by the side closest to the waterfall and ducked behind a large potted fern. She was right. Water puddled down her feet and ran across the floor. It was a good thing she wasn't wearing shoes, or she might have been making squeaky noises as she walked. Mina did the best she could to wring out her wet shirt into the fern. It started to move and sway at her watery offering.

"Psst, no," she shushed the plant. But its fronds tried to reach for her as if giving her a hug. "Gah, no! You don't have to say thank you." She stepped away, and the fern wilted a little, as if she'd hurt its feelings. "Are you going to be nice and stay still this time?" The plant wiggled in anticipation, but it looked like it said yes. "Then be good." Mina finished wringing out her shirt and hair, and did the best she could with her pants. There was still a puddle forming whenever she walked, but at least it was a small one.

Someone was coming from down the hall, and Mina ducked behind the fern once more. This time the plant wrapped its large fronds around her, not to hug her but to help hide her.

It was a guard, in full white leather armor, unlike the giants and the trolls outside. This one was covered in head-to-toe steel with emblems of the sun and moon etched across his breastplate. He was running toward the end of the hall, where two huge double doors opened before he even got there. Her heart leapt for joy when she saw Jared step out and confront the soldier. No, wait, she had to remember that they only looked similar. It wasn't Jared—it was his brother Teague, dressed all in black.

"What is it, Captain Plaith?" Teague demanded angrily.

"Something has agitated the trolls and giants, my prince. Even the siren went off."

Teague froze at the words of his captain and glared at him. "And..."

"And kelpies, sire. They were seen causing a ruckus near the palace." The guard fidgeted but was careful to stare at a spot to the left of the prince."

Fable

"Kelpies? That's it? Those stupid water horses are always causing a ruckus. Anything else?"

"No, sire. Just that there were two kelpies seen outside in the lake."

Teague sighed and rubbed his forehead. "There are always kelpies in the lake. Tell your men to get back to your stations." Teague shooed off his captain and headed down a long hall, but then he stopped and turned around, and called back his captain.

"Plaith?"

"Yes, my prince." The tall man shuffled forward once more.

"Did you say that there were only two kelpies?"

"Yes, two. One on land and one in the water."

Teague stared toward the waterfall and then the fountain in thought. His dark eyes missed nothing as he scanned the room, and spent an awful lot of time staring directly at the planter she was hiding behind. Her legs started to shake from fear. Even the fern began to quiver.

"There are never just two kelpies. They travel in herds," Teague said thoughtfully. "Where's the rest of the herd? You also said the underwater siren went off?"

The soldier nodded.

Teague looked pleased with himself. "Double the giants and the trolls at the gates, and bring more guards to each of the walls just in case. I believe we have company."

237

"But sire, if there is something in the castle that is a threat to the Fates, shouldn't we notify—"

Teague's blue eyes blazed with fury. His hand lifted to strike the soldier, but Plaith flinched and Teague restrained himself. "Don't question my authority again. The Fates are at the Twilight Festival and won't be back till later. There is nothing here that could possibly be a threat to the Fates. Now go!" He pointed, and Plaith fled. But Teague didn't leave; he stood, frozen, looking back at the potted fern.

"There's nothing or no one here that could possibly hurt the Fates—right, Mina?"

Twenty~Five

She froze and let his voice echo in the empty hall. Maybe if she held her breath and closed her eyes, he would disappear like a bad dream. He didn't. The plant began to shake even more, as if it was afraid of the prince, and she put a hand on its fronds to calm it down. This was ridiculous. She shouldn't be afraid of Teague—she wasn't before. This time she had nothing—no Grimoire, no phoenix feather, and no shard of magic glass—to defend herself with. Only her wits.

"Come, Mina, you must be freezing. Let's get you warmed up, and then we will talk." Teague gestured down the hall, and she still stood rooted to the spot. His eyes turned dark, and his voice dripped with venom. "I said, come here."

He whipped his finger in her direction, and the large potted fern she was hiding behind was flung across the room and smashed into pieces on the stone wall. She cried out when the plant struggled once and then quit moving. Whatever magic was within it quickly died, and the plant just became a plant. In that one moment she understood a little bit more about the Fae magic and how it worked.

"It's not like you to hide."

"It's not like you to steal and lie, no, wait—it is." She smirked, filling her voice with false bravado.

Teague shook his head and let his dark hair settle over his forehead. He was handsome—not as handsome as Jared, because she could see it now, more so since she was on the Fae plane. He was able to hide it whenever he visited the physical plane, but here, Teague couldn't hide the darkness that was attached to his soul, put there by the splitting of the books. One brother good, the other evil. Granted, there were a few times that she thought Jared could be the evil one, but standing here, face to face, with no cloaking, glamour or magic, she could see the true Story. And it scared her to her very core.

"I want what is mine," she demanded. "I want my brother."

"Oh, Mina, you can't have him. You haven't completed your quest. You know the rules as well as I. You must complete the Story. Only then can you have what you so desire." He walked away from her, down the darkened hall.

How dare he walk away from her! She took off running after him, but stopped when she came to the broken plant. It was silly of her, and she knew it, but she couldn't help but want to touch it and thank it for trying to help her. Her hands stroked its large fronds, and she whispered, "I'm sorry. It's not fair! But thank you for giving your life for me." She stood to leave, and didn't notice that after she walked away, the plant began to grow again. It slowly reached one frond after her, and then she was gone.

Teague walked out of the bathing room and into a large sitting room that looked to be connected to another larger suite of rooms. He pulled the leaf of a small blue bell, and a chiming sound could be heard in the distance. A few moments later a small Fae scurried in wearing a pale blue dress and a silver moon on a sash.

"Bring the girl some clothes and bandages," Teague ordered, and then walked to a small table and poured himself a drink and offered Mina some.

She shook her head and he smiled, but the smile didn't reach his lips. "Someone has taught you well."

Mina couldn't help but raise her chin and smile.

"But obviously it wasn't enough, because I don't see Jared." Teague sighed. "He is such a coward."

"He's not a coward. You're the coward. Kidnapping young innocent boys, burning my home down because you're scared of me. You're scared of what I'm going to do to you."

"He's not an innocent," Teague said stiffly.

"He's a child, a nine-year-old boy."

"He's a Grimm." Teague gave her a look, daring her to argue that point with her.

"I'm a Grimm! If you have a problem, come after me, not my brother."

"Oh, Mina, you are so fun to play with. I tried to get you to play, but you ignored the quests, and you know that's not how we play nice. So I need to get you interested in the game again."

She was about to say something when the servant appeared with clothes for her to change into. There was a dress of deep red, and what looked like stockings and slippers. Mina picked up the dress and unconsciously made a face in disgust at the color choice.

Teague laughed hard at her expression. "Oh, that was a good one. I remember turning all of your clothes red for the Riding Hood Tale. To this day you still don't wear the color red, do you?" He continued to laugh so hard that he wiped a tear away from the corner of his eye. "Oh, yes, that has been my favorite quest to date."

She stared daggers at Teague, and finally he calmed down and walked over to the dress. "All right, what would you like it to be?" He snapped his fingers. "Blue, emerald, white." With each color he named, the dress turned the matching color. "Or how about your newest favorite—gold." He left off on that color and watched Mina closely to see her reaction.

She flinched but refused to make a sound. Teague left the dress a pale shimmering gold, and pointed to a delicate screen for her to change behind. This was stupid, she thought. Even though she was freezing and dripping wet, the outfit she had on was much more suited to escaping than a dress.

"Thank you, but no." She stepped away from him and dropped the dress on a chair.

Teague wasn't amused. "You should be beheaded for trespassing. I still could have you killed, but instead I thought it would be fitting to try to be nice. The least you can do is not insult your host," His words were soft-spoken, befitting his royal status, but every word dripped with his wrath.

She could feel the full force of his ire, and her hands shook with trepidation. She picked up the dress, stockings, and slippers, and ducked behind the screen. By the time she was getting into the dress, she was no longer scared but furious. How dare he play with her like she was a pawn in a game. *Does he not know that even a pawn can take down the queen?* Thought after thought plagued Mina, and she was slowly building up enough anger that she could feel her body trembling, but this time it was with power. There was a full-length mirror behind the screen, and she could see herself in it. Her hair, a wet tangled mess, fell over one shoulder. Her skin looked pale, and her eyes burned with anger. The dress was frilly, stupid frilly and too long, and rubbed against her bandaged leg. The slippers were impractical, with silk on the soles. She was dressed up like a doll, and she felt like she was ten years old. It was then that she realized this wasn't to help her but to make her feel demoralized, weak. And she wasn't that. Never that.

"Oh, for heaven's sake. This dress and shoes have got to go," she grumbled as she tried to brush out her hair. The power that had gathered around her flowed to her almost excitedly and answered her deepest desire. The dress shimmered and glowed, the long skirts shrinking away to become formfitting pants in a soft tan color. The top of the gown became a long-sleeved shirt of the palest white, and a brown belt appeared around her hips. She was doing it again, unconsciously controlling Fae magic. The slippers grew longer and ran up her calves until she was wearing knee-high boots. Even her hair had dried and was plaited in a braid over her shoulder.

She smiled at her reflection and whispered, *Thank you*, to the unseen magic. She really needed to work at becoming more attuned to calling it, and feeling when it was near. Feeling confident, Mina walked around the screen, only to find Teague confused and speechless.

"Wha…how? I didn't give you those clothes."

"Yes, you did. I just changed them to suit my needs," Mina quipped.

"But how?" He stared at her in disbelief, and then his expression changed to one of joy. And not the happy joy, either. He turned, and she could see him become even more excited. "I knew you were the right one. I just knew." He held out his arm and waited for her to join him. "Come, I think there is someone you are dying to meet."

Fable

Mina didn't need any more prompting but hurried after Teague, afraid that he would change his mind and decide to not take her to Charlie.

He didn't. They walked through three different-colored corridors, a sky blue, a golden yellow, and a soft lavender, before they entered what appeared to be the north wing of the palace. The hall was a dismal gray, the colors on the tapestries faded and drab, and even the rugs looked neglected, as if this was the wing that life had forgotten. In a palace of sun and moon and light, this wing reeked of darkness and death.

Teague came to a set of black double doors with a dead tree burned into the wood grain. Teague raised his right hand over a round metal sphere, and Mina knew it was another magical seal. A bright buzzing glow, a pop, and the sound of a lever clicking unlocked the seal. The doors opened inward, and they entered the room.

It was dark, with a pale hint of the moons' glow coming in through the glass ceiling. It took a few moments for her eyes to adjust. The room was as big as her high school auditorium; the walls were lined with tall pillars of white marble. In the middle of the room on a golden pedestal illuminated by the moon was a book. She didn't need any explanation to know that this was the Fae's book.

It was large and old, and there was a resonant hum that seemed to be coming from the book, or maybe it was her imagination. As soon as she stepped into the room, the large double doors shut behind her, and a huge crossbeam slid into place, locking it. A faint purple glow appeared around the doors, and Mina knew that Teague had magically as well as physically sealed them in the room.

Teague went right up to the Fae book and placed his hand on it lovingly. He closed his eyes, and his hair began to blow around the room. It looked like he had just become stronger from touching the book. There was a large stone fireplace at one end of the room, with two wooden throne-like chairs on the other. Another fountain trickled soothingly by a wall of large glass windows. It looked like the room at one time had been a ballroom.

"So here it is, Mina. The book. I know about the Stiltskin's backhanded deal with you to steal this book for your brother. But let me just tell you, stealing the book for him won't complete the quest."

Mina barely listened to Teague's monologue as she scanned the room. There in the corner she saw it. A golden cage.

"Charlie!" she screamed, and ran to the prison. Charlie was cuddled up in the blankets just like in her dream, and he awoke to the sound of her voice. He flung off the blanket and reached his hands through the bars toward his sister.

"Oh, Charlie, sweetie. I'm so sorry I didn't protect you. I'll get you out of here, I promise." Mina's hands touched his face, his head, and then his arms, checking to see if he was hurt.

Charlie's fingers dug deeply into Mina's arms, and silent tears trickled down his cheeks. He pressed his little face against the bars to try to get as close to her as he could. Fresh tears poured down Mina's face, but she ignored them.

Mina stood up and went to the lock on the cage. It looked to be a mixture of a combination lock and a magical seal.

"Unlock it...NOW." Her voice left little room for argument.

"I can't. You haven't finished your tale. You must defeat the Stiltskin to win back your brother."

"But I already have. I trapped the copper Stiltskin in the Grimoire. What more do you want?" she cried out, refusing to let go of her brother.

Teague walked over to a hidden door in the wall and opened it. On the other side was Temple Stiltskin, and he looked furious. His boots clicked ominously as he walked into the middle of the room and glared at Mina.

"You said you had nothing to do with Reid's disappearance!" Temple roared, his hands flexing ominously by his sides. "You lied."

"Not on purpose. He attacked me, and I had to defend myself. I'm not even sure why he was there. I was already on a quest with you," Mina said, trying to explain.

Temple froze and turned to stare at Teague. "Did you send my youngest brother to fight a Grimm after I had already promised I would steal the boy for you? Why? I made the bargain—I said I would put together the quest for you. Why in all our worlds would you do something so underhanded?"

It was obvious that even Temple was operating in an unhappy work environment. Something was falling apart between them, and it wasn't the most beneficial relationship.

Teague walked away from his beloved book and raised his hands in the air. "He was tired of being the youngest, the weakest. He wanted fame and glory, and came to me. He offered his services to me, and since our Grimm wasn't in any hurry to try to save her brother, I thought I would give her a warning."

Temple raised his hands and let out a truly broken-hearted cry.

Teague looked bored and began to tap his fingers together in impatience. "So Mina, here he is—your tale. Defeat him, and I will give you back what you have lost. Lose, and the curse will most definitely pass to him."

"NO! You can't do that!" she spat at him, and stood up to face the Stiltskin, then had a moment's hesitation.

"Temple, now remember, it wasn't I who killed your brother, but the girl. That is at least a parting gift I can give you." Teague smiled wanly.

Temple's eyes were red from crying, but he turned to Mina with fury burning brightly in his eyes. "I will kill you for my brother!" He flung open his jacket and pulled forth a small vial. He opened it up and dropped a small golden fang into the palm of his hand. He whispered something in the Fae language, and

Fable

the fang grew longer and longer till it couldn't be contained in his palm anymore. The tip of the fang reared its head, and a reptilian hood appeared around it. Mina could see two blood-red eyes staring at her as the fang morphed and continued to grow into a large golden cobra.

"One of my pets would like to say hello," Temple bragged.

She sucked in her breath in fright and looked around the room for a weapon. Anything with which to fight off the cobra. The snake slithered along the ground, now as tall as a full-grown human and intent on making her its next victim. Teague had moved over to a large chair by the book and sat down in it, watching the forthcoming battle with interest. His fingers drummed along the armrest as if he was becoming impatient.

Mina ran away from the middle of the room, and grabbed a large vase and threw it at the snake. It saw the attack and quickly moved out of the way of the vessel, which crashed and splintered along the marble floor. She ran toward the fireplace and grabbed the long fire poker, and spun around just as the cobra lunged at her.

Her hand went up reflexively and she swung the poker, knocking the snake's attack to the side. He had missed—barely. The cobra was angry and coiled himself protectively before he raised his head, which was as large as a Doberman, and swayed back and forth. His large hood opened in an attempt to intimidate her. It worked.

Her hands shook, and she could feel the handle of the metal poker digging into her skin because of her deathly grip on it. The snake lunged at her again, and she stepped to the side and used the poker to stab furiously at the cobra. She did it—she stabbed the snake, but her aim was off and she missed the head. In retaliation, the snake whipped its tail around and knocked Mina's only weapon across the floor.

She watched as the poker skidded to a halt by a column. The snake was fast, faster than she had anticipated, and she didn't have the help of the Grimoire or Jared. But it didn't mean that she was completely defenseless. She glanced over at the book sitting behind Teague, and an idea began to form in her head. It was a stupid idea, but stupid ideas worked the best— well, at least for her, anyway.

Mina turned and began to lead the snake back toward Teague. It followed. She began to run, and it took after her. She jumped up onto the podium, and as soon as she grabbed the book, two large strong hands grabbed her from behind and lifted her bodily into the air. It was Temple. She had temporarily forgotten about the Stiltskin. This fight wasn't fair—it was two against one.

Mina screamed as her legs flew into the air and couldn't find purchase. Temple was stronger than he looked as he began to squeeze her body. She felt like candy, brittle between his arms. She choked and couldn't catch her breath.

Fable

Teague sat unmoving in his chair, not amused. He didn't even seem surprised when she'd tried to make a play for the book. His fingers drummed across the armrest impatiently.

"Help!" she tried to choke out, but the word died on her lips, and he squeezed again. A rattling noise reached her ears, and she felt her whole world freeze. Temple turned her toward the large man-sized snake and held her out like an offering. The snake slithered angrily toward her, blood dripping from its wound. It was twenty feet away, ten feet away, five—when a loud crackle and burst of light appeared.

Everyone's head whipped to the large double doors. Bright white light leaked through the cracks of the door as the magic seal was unlocked. There was still a huge crossbeam that physically locked the door, but whoever was on the other side wasn't letting that stand in the way.

A crashing boom rocked the room, and the chandeliers began to shake. Vases skittered a few inches off the tables. The crash came again and again, and the beam cracked in the smallest spot. Teague stood up in amazement and stared at the door. Temple refused to put her down, but even the snake had turned at the sound of the new threat.

Crash! The doors blew off their iron hinges, and everyone had to duck as pieces of wood, metal, and doorframe flew every which way. The dust had barely cleared when Nix ran into the room. He looked deathly pale, and his hair was turning an odd brown shade. His green eyes had faded to an almost gray color, but that wasn't what surprised her the most—it was who was on his heels.

One of the largest giants Mina had ever seen lumbered through the broken doors, smashing what was left of them under his feet. He looked like one of the giants who'd been guarding the bridge, but she couldn't be sure.

"Mina!" Nix yelled, and ran toward her.

The snake quickly turned back and rose up again to strike. This time he was closer to her, and Temple grabbed Mina's forehead and pulled it roughly toward the ceiling, exposing her neck. She swallowed, and felt the snake's eyes zero in on the soft skin of throat and her Adam's apple. It hissed, and its jaw opened wide. Maybe she imagined it, but she thought she saw a drip of venom slide off its perfectly gold fang.

She heard herself let out a little whimper, and she closed her eyes as it lunged forward. Something hard thudded against her, and she felt pain around her throat. She imagined it was the snake wrapping itself around her and biting her.

A groan was heard behind her, and then she was falling, falling to the ground. She smacked the marble floor and rolled away. Mina opened her eyes to see that it was Nix who was now wrapped up in a battle for life or death with the cobra. He had something in his hand and he tried to use it to stab the snake, but it was knocked from his hand and skittered across the floor to land right in front of Mina.

Fable

It was her knife. Temple was lying on the floor, bleeding, clutching his head where a large cut had appeared, a broken vase lying next to him. The large giant who had barreled through the door was now being flung across the room into the marble wall. Huge web-like cracks spiraled out of the marble in every direction.

Teague had stood up and was laughing hysterically—finally enjoying the battle, it seemed. He looked pleased to have worthy opponents. Mina didn't give the giant any other thought, but lunged for the glass knife and went to help Nix.

She was almost there when she saw the snake rear its head back for a strike, and then he bit Nix in the shoulder. She heard him scream! It was the most awful heart-wrenching noise, and then she realized it wasn't Nix who was screaming—she was!

Mina leapt onto the snake's back, and stabbed it over and over and over again. It didn't matter; on the first strike, the snake began to writhe in pain as it slowly turned to gold. She dropped the shard of glass and quickly pulled Nix out of the snake's grasp before he was stuck in a golden snake coffin.

"Nix! Are you okay?" Mina cried out, using her hands to cover up the large nickel-sized holes in his shoulders.

His skin was drying out, and his eyes looked almost white now. "I'm sorry I didn't come sooner. I'm sorry that I didn't help save your brother. I'm sorry that I am a poor excuse for a nixie."

"You said so yourself that nixies are gentle creatures. I should never have asked you to help me on this quest. And now it's all my fault that you are dying."

"I was always dying. Now I have done something brave before I died. I am happy." His breathing slowed, and Mina tried to make him comfortable. Her heart was hurting so badly with guilt she was finding it hard to breathe.

A large roar filled the air, and a table flew past her head. She screamed and covered Nix's body with hers to protect him, and looked up in alarm. Charlie was wringing the bars of his cage frantically and pointing at the Stiltskin. Temple had finally gotten over his disorientation, because he was opening up his jacket and pulling something else out of his jacket. A golden feather.

A screech echoed through the room, and the phoenix once again appeared, flying high in the air. Temple spun the feather in a circle around the room, and the phoenix flew the same path, creating a circle of fire that split the room in two, with Charlie on one side of the five-foot-tall flame and Mina on the other.

It was just like her dream. Mina watched the phoenix fly out of reach and sit on a tall crossbeam. She couldn't help but feel sorry for the firebird, and then her heart constricted even more when she realized how little choice Stiltskin's slaves had in the matter. The firebird and snake didn't want to be slaves any more than she did. What in the world would a Stiltskin do if he had a Grimm as a slave?

Fable

"Charlie!" Mina called out to him through the smoke and flame. She could barely see him through the wall of fire. She had to defeat the Stiltskin, and then she had to save her brother and find a way back to her own world.

She grabbed the shard of glass and ran back to the Fae book. Teague had left the book unattended as he fought the giant. Her eyes looked for him in the room, and she realized that Teague as a Royal had morphed into a giant saber-tooth tiger and was slashing the giant across the chest with his large claws. The giant let out a long, painful roar, and she was distracted once again. There she stood in front of the Fae book and she had it in her hands, but she couldn't pull herself away from the giant's plight.

The giant reached out and grabbed the saber-tooth by the back of the neck, and flung it across the room. The cat nimbly landed on his paws and then shape-shifted back into the young handsome Teague, who looked winded and had a smear of blood coming out of his mouth.

"Very good, brother. I am impressed. You have gotten stronger, but you are not strong enough."

Brother? The word made Mina's knees weak with relief. It couldn't be—could it? He said he would never come. That he couldn't come. She couldn't help herself; she yelled out his name. "Jared!"

The giant's head turned to her, his eyes looking very human and every ounce Jared. He had one hand over a deep wound in

255

his side, and he was slowly falling to his knees. She heard him call out her name—"Meehna!"—and then he fell forward onto the marble. But when he finally crashed into the ground, he was completely human and injured.

Teague danced over to his brother's body and kicked him in the stomach. Jared curled up into a ball, and then, slowly, ever so slowly, he got back up to his feet. His hair was tousled, his clothes torn, and even in his human form, the injuries translated into large slashes crisscrossed across his chest and face. And even though his brother taunted him, Jared never took his eyes off her.

Her heart soared! He'd come for her! He hadn't abandoned her. She was going to have quite a few angry words with him later, but for now, since her Jared was here, she knew they would be all right.

Jared's hands going up in the air and his eyes widening in fright were Mina's only warning that something was wrong. She turned just as Temple's ungloved hand reached for her arm.

Her arm swung up, and she stabbed Temple in the palm of the hand with the piece of the glass knife. Temple screamed and stepped back, holding his bleeding hand. He stared at the golden glass in horror and then at the blood that dripped from the wound. It was first red, and then slowly, drip by drip, it turned to gold. He pulled out the glass and dropped it in shock.

"No! No! What have you done? How did you know?"

Mina stared at him without any sympathy. "A deal made in blood that can only be broken by blood. Yours."

"How could you have come by my blood?" He groaned in pain, trying to use his power to reverse the effect of the magic that was turning his arm and shoulder into gold. He was able to change it back for a second, but then he would be overwhelmed and lose the ground he'd gained. He was sweating and fighting it so hard. Mina knew he would lose the battle.

"You gave it to me…freely."

"I would have done no such thiii—" And he was gone. The most powerful Stiltskin encased in his own golden curse. And she'd done it without the Grimoire.

A loud screeching noise came from the ceiling, and the phoenix flexed its wings and flew in a giant circle. *Thank you for freeing me,* the voice echoed in Mina's head. The bird flew over her head, making Teague duck for cover, and in a wink of an eye, all of the flames in the room were gone. The bird came to light on Teague's book and looked at Mina with large solemn eyes.

"You're welcome, but now can you help me?" Mina turned to point to Nix, whose shoulder had turned a deep purple color. He was gasping for each and every breath. "They say that a phoenix's tears can heal people. Is that true?"

"Yes, but even if I heal him, he will still die on this plane."

"So there's nothing you can do?" Mina cried out. A warm arm wrapped around her shoulder, and she could feel Jared coming to aid her.

"*No, there's nothing I can do. I am truly sorry,*" the bird said, using tones of her mother's anguished voice. "*But I thank you again for our freedom.*"

"Our?" Mina looked around, confused.

"*Your bravery not only freed me, it freed all of those entrapped by his malicious deals.*" The phoenix's voice became deeper, more masculine. The timbre of the familiar voice made Mina go weak in the knees. The voice of her father. The bird looked toward the Stiltskin, who was surrounded by gold orbs that grew and grew until they took the shape of their true form.

A small gold bubble phased into a young tree nymph who looked around the room and took off running down the hall. An even larger orb phased into a dazed and confused griffin. Another released an ogre, a small fairy. One after another, hundreds of orbs shifted, and Fae of all races and sizes began to walk among each other, hugging one another and rejoicing in their freedom. Then the most amazing thing happened as each and every one of the freed Fae bowed toward Mina in respect.

Teague walked back and forth, his anger spilling off him in waves. "No, no, no! You shouldn't be bowing to her—I'm the one who freed you. I sent the Stiltskin into her world so she could defeat him. I'm the one who instigated the quest! You should bow to me!"

Fable

The menagerie of freed slaves ignored Teague and departed through all available exits, out of the broken windows, the destroyed walls into the courtyard, and even into the palace itself, eager to leave and not be enslaved again. The phoenix called out to her in one truly earsplitting scream of joy and then vanished into the night.

But there was one golden orb left. It was the last to be released and the slowest to be freed. The final orb floated farther away from her, to the middle of the floor, and slowly phased into the form of a man who looked familiar. It couldn't be...could it?

He looked confused, dazed, and stumbled over a broken column. His dull brown hair and small moustache couldn't hide the wide fear-ridden brown eyes as the man stared at the Stiltskin statue in horror.

"No, it can't be," Mina choked out and froze, her hand going to her heart as she tried to call out his name. She hadn't seen him in almost nine years, so she couldn't be certain, was too scared in case she was wrong. Mina tried to say something, but his name died on her lips, barely a squeak. "Father?"

But he was gone; he made his escape, like the others, into the night. She was about to run after him into the Fae world, but she couldn't—not yet. She had a duty here...now. A quest to finish, and she couldn't be sure it was him. Maybe she only imagined it was him because the phoenix had just spoken to her using his voice.

"Come on, Mina," Jared's soft voice whispered into her ear. His arm wrapped around her and she buried herself in his embrace.

"You came?" She started to cry soft, silent tears.

"I'm not supposed to come back. My mother the Queen forbade it—she said it was too dangerous for me here. So I was banished to your world, never to cross over, for fear of my life."

"Why did you come? I-I thought you were angry at me for coming, and you said you wouldn't follow." She started to hiccup.

Jared's gray eyes bored into hers. His face filled with emotion, and his own eyes looked to be just as tear-filled. "Do you really not know the reason why I came? I came back for you. I'll always come back for you."

He pressed his forehead to hers. His nearness tickled her senses, and she couldn't help but hold him even tighter. Jared gently tipped Mina's chin up, and he leaned down to press his lips to hers in a soft kiss that quickly turned into desire. So many pent-up emotions and unsaid words spilled out between them in a kiss to top all kisses. Never before had she lost all sense of time and place as her lips sought after those of her protector, her friend and her Fae prince. All thoughts of Brody disappeared as her world encompassed Jared and Jared only.

Fable

He pulled away, and he was visibly shaking from the intensity of their kiss. "Mina, I want you to know that I've felt alone for a very long time. I was incomplete, and nothing could fill that void. Until I met you. I've known for a long time, but I wasn't sure how you felt about me. At times I thought you hated me, but I wanted to tell you that I, uh, Mina, I lo—aaaarrgh!"

Jared's body tensed up in pain, and he fell away from her. Mina tried to grab him and pull him close, but something stabbed her in the side. She looked down and saw her torso covered with blood, but it wasn't hers. She looked up to see a large knife sticking out of Jared's stomach. Teague stood behind him with his hand wrapped around Jared's throat, his eyes glittering evilly.

Twenty~Six

Jared's eyes were squeezed shut in pain, but he refused to make a noise.

"Teague, no, let him go," Mina begged. Jared's eyes opened wide, and he shook his head from side to side, telling her to keep quiet.

"That's right. Mother dearest sent him to the human world to keep him from me." He still had the knife inside Jared, and he hadn't pulled it out yet. That knife was the only thing keeping him from bleeding out. "She knew how much I needed him," Teague raged wildly.

"I don't understand!" Mina cried out, her hands clenched at her side in anger.

"It's easy, Mina. I want power! I want you to finish more quests so I become more powerful. Use the book. Use my book to entrap them all." Teague giggled madly. He was becoming unstable. She could see him flinching and blinking like an addict searching for his next fix.

"I can't," she whispered.

"Yes, you can. It's easy. It's the same as your book. Just open its pages and finish the tale."

Mina slowly walked through the rubble of the room, toward the podium. She kept glancing between Charlie, who was being very brave and watching from inside his cage, to Jared, whose face had now broken out in a sweat. He was doing his very best to stay calm and not worry her, but his eyes kept flicking to her brother.

Why would Teague want to hurt Jared? Why would he need her to use the Fae book? Was it all part of his giant plan to gain more power? Why was Jared so worried about Charlie?

"Not until you release my brother," Mina said firmly. She knew that no matter what happened, he needed to be safe.

Teague's eyes narrowed, and he wiggled the knife inside Jared, who groaned and bit his lip to keep from crying out.

Mina stood tall, the tears still coming, but she refused to waver. "LET MY BROTHER GO! I defeated your quest! I want my brother, now!"

"Very well." Teague waved his finger, and the lock clicked off Charlie's cage. The small boy ran to Mina and clutched her around the waist. Mina knew that now was not the time to be distracted again. She pulled Charlie with her and looked upon the Fae book for the very first time.

She had been told that at one time there was only one book, and that a Fae had split the book in two: one with the power for good, the other for evil, and that whatever quest or tale the Grimms completed on the physical plane, it would magically appear in the Fae book. Here she had the chance to look upon it with her own eyes, and she gasped.

The Fae book was definitely filled with the same stories as hers, but this one was filled with picture after picture of Jared. She couldn't help but flip backward a few pages and see magical images come to life: of Jared defending her in an alley. Sitting in art class with Mina, spinning on the pottery wheel. There was another one of Jared by the lake, teaching her to fight. Jared and her in the storage room, laughing, before their tickling fight. She flipped forward and saw the last page filled with a motion-captured image of Jared and her sharing a kiss.

"What is this?" There was something terribly wrong, a feeling deep in the pit of her stomach that this wasn't right. It wasn't the same as the pictures in her Grimoire.

"Use the Fae book and finish the quest, Mina. Or I'll kill Jared."

"Mina, don't do it. Just take your brother and run," Jared hissed as his brother squeezed more tightly around his throat.

"I can't get back, Jared. I never figured out how to get back on my own."

Jared's gaze flickered down to his pocket, and one hand slowly reached down to pull something out of it. It was small and silver, and it fit in the palm of his hand. "I had to go to the old biddies and have them fix it, but it's yours. It should have always been yours." He flung the seam ripper as hard as he could toward Mina, and he screamed as Teague pulled the knife out at the same time. Jared collapsed on the ground, holding his side, and slowly his fingers turned red with blood.

The seam ripper came to rest by her boot. Charlie picked it up in his hands and stood protectively by Mina's side.

"Now you have no choice, Mina. Use the Fae book, or Jared will die...here...right now."

"Okay!" She spun around in anger and lifted the book high into the air above her. She flipped open a blank page, and turned it toward the golden body of Temple and the snake. Nothing happened. "Why aren't you working?"

Teague turned to her, his arms opening wide; he dropped the knife onto the floor and smiled widely. "Because that is not the quest I've set up for you. You need to use it on me—on us." He started to spin widely in a circle. "I've waited hundreds of years, brother, for this moment. To finally have you and a Grimm in the same place, and now I've done it. The other Grimms didn't entice you enough to come back to our world. But you never expected me to pick a girl, did you? And one that you would fall in love with."

Mina stared at them and felt numb. Teague wanted Jared. It was always about Jared. He manipulated Temple to steal her brother, knowing Mina would come here, and eventually Jared would follow. It was a trap, and she was the bait, and now Jared was going to die because of her.

"Miiinna, Miiinna. You're wasting valuable time. He's dying, Mina, and it's all your fault. Just complete this final tale, and you can save him."

"Are you sure?"

"Yes, he's my brother, my other half, and I want what is best for him. I've always wanted what is best for him. But what kind of hero are you if you can't even save the one you love? You do love him, Mina, don't you? I'm sure in that small, confused, easily swayed human heart, there beats some love for this Fae."

"But the book, it could…what if it..?"

"The books have been a part of us for so long, it won't hurt us. I promise. It's the only thing that can heal us." Teague held his hand out to her. "We've been torn apart for so long, you are the only one who can truly heal us."

Her heart started to race, and she gripped the pages of the book so hard she could feel them wrinkle in her fingers. She was angry, angry at being tricked, angry at being used. But she wouldn't let her own feelings get in the way of saving Jared's life. She at least owed that to him.

Mina pulled all of the magic in the room toward her and let it flood her. She was furious and she wanted Teague to pay, but she wanted Jared to live more. She felt a guttural scream rip forth, and she forced all of the power through her and into the book. She flipped open the book to a blank page and turned it on Teague.

He was so sure it was the only way to save Jared, and she didn't have any other choice. Jared had stopped moving on the floor.

A bright light burst forth from the book and shot straight into Teague's heart, while another beam of light poured into Jared's dying form on the ground. They both began to glow brighter and brighter. Teague began to laugh maniacally, his body slowly raised off the floor until he was floating in the air. Jared's unconscious body lifted into the air and floated next to Teague's. Mina could see the wound on Jared's abdomen slowly start to heal itself. Teague was right. The book was healing them and not entrapping them within its pages.

She began to have hope and kept pouring every ounce of power she could into directing the book. She didn't know what she was supposed to be doing, but obviously the Fae book did.

Jared groaned and opened his eyes. When he saw himself floating in the air and the beam of light going into his heart, he began to struggle and yell. "NOOOO, noo!"

It was only then that she questioned her choice. Teague had lied.

"Mina!" Jared cried out, and reached for her.

She dropped the book, but it never hit the floor. It continued to float and send vivid beams of light and power into the two brothers. But then something began to happen. The brothers began to be drawn closer together, and the light grew brighter and brighter. Threads of power wrapped around them, binding them, and then both Jared and Teague converged into one.

A retinue of guards rushed into the ballroom, followed by the Fates, the royal King and Queen. Queen Maeve screamed out No before falling to the ground in a faint.

A loud noise filled the room, and threads of magic lashed out in every direction, knocking anyone who was standing to the ground. It took Mina a few seconds to gather her thoughts, for she was blinded and couldn't hear. She looked to the middle of the blast area where Jared and Teague were last. She could only see one body, and it was lying prone on the floor. The body moved and groaned, and Mina knew it was Jared.

Twenty~Seven

Mina ran to the body on the floor and flipped Jared over, and wrapped her arms around him.

"You're okay. You're alive," she whispered, and ran her hands over his face. Jared's eyes fluttered open, and she sat back on her heels in shock. The young man before her was Jared. It had Jared's hair, face, body, but the eyes were wrong. They weren't gray, they were blue—like Teague's.

"What, no kiss?" he sneered, and pushed her hand away in disgust. He sat up and looked around the room, and began to laugh.

Queen Maeve, her dark raven hair stunning against her white dress, looked even paler from the distress of what she had just witnessed. Even King Lucian appeared shocked at what had transpired. He held onto his beautiful wife and spoke quietly to the royal guards behind him.

Teague turned to the Queen and said, "Well, hello, Mother," and laughed when she took a step back from him in fright.

What had she done? Mina felt a hand pull against her arm and looked at a stricken Charlie. He kept pointing and dragging her away. She followed her brother to the other side of the room and couldn't help but feel that she had just done the worst thing imaginable. She had destroyed Jared. Yes, he was now alive, but that person, that thing across the room was not her Jared.

Her feet were filled with lead, and she kept stumbling and tripping as they ran through the rubble. Charlie stopped by a still form and knelt down. Nix was still breathing! Mina grabbed his hands and felt a gentle squeeze back from Nix. His face was now almost unrecognizable from the swelling, and she could see he had almost stopped breathing.

"You are the bravest nixie ever. Thank you for choosing to not give in to your curse," Mina whispered.

Nix could no longer speak, but he blinked back in response. A huge tear slid down his face.

Charlie handed Mina the seam ripper, and she didn't hesitate for one second. She pressed the gem on the end, and a pop and crackle emanated from the tip. Mina quickly mimicked Ever and drew a large circle in the air. The seam ripper continued to pop and ripple as it cut through the planes, creating a door. The door wavered and then turned lucid. She could see something on the other side, and it looked like her world.

270

"Charlie, you go first!" she commanded, but he was nowhere near the portal. Instead, her silent brother was holding onto Nix's arm and trying to drag him toward the opening. "Charlie, we can't help him."

The little nine-year-old boy put his hands on his hips and glared at her. She knew that look, knew that Charlie wouldn't budge without bringing Nix along.

"Okay, fine." Mina could see that the gate was slowly closing, and she couldn't waste any more time. She leaned down and put Nix's arm over her shoulder, and half dragged, half carried him toward the portal. Once Charlie had seen that he had gotten his way, he happily jumped through the gate into their world.

Mina couldn't help it. She turned to look at the Fae world one last time. A battle had ensued between Jared/Teague and the guards. Being a Royal meant that they were both shifters, and now that the two were one, he was an even stronger and more ruthless fighter. She heard a scream and a sword flew past her face, and she knew then she needed to leave.

She took a deep breath and dipped down to get better grip on Nix. She heard him whisper in awe as he looked at the gate, "Is this Heaven?"

"No, but it's as close as we get," Mina answered before jumping through the gate.

Twenty~Eight

She awoke back in the biology lab. Something wet was pressed against her face, and she sat up abruptly to wipe it away. She had been drooling. Soft whispers and giggles erupted around her, and Mina sat back in the chair and stared at everyone in confusion.

She was sitting at an empty lab table at the back of the room, and the rest of the class seemed to be in the middle of a lab experiment.

A familiar face popped in front of her, and Melissa smiled sweetly before whispering loudly, "So are you thinking of retaking biology? I hear it can get pretty gross." She had sneaked over to Mina's empty table. Her friends were looking at Mina and waving. They were the source of the giggles. "I didn't even know you were here. One minute this table is empty. The next, you're here. Are you, like, related to Houdini?"

"No, where am I?" Mina asked worriedly. She spun around in her chair and then hopped off to look underneath the lab table for Charlie.

"Um, last period," Melissa answered, and ducked under the lab table with Mina.

Luckily, most of the class seemed preoccupied with working, and the teacher didn't notice the sudden appearance of an extra upperclassman student in their class.

"Well, what day is today?" Mina felt completely at a loss. What had happened? Where was Charlie? Where was Nix?

Melissa frowned and then gently touched Mina's head. "You don't look so good. Maybe you should head out to see the nurse. I'd use the back door, since you don't want to get detention. I'm pretty sure I can cause a distraction, and you can slip out."

"Can you?" Mina asked, relieved.

"No problem." Melissa popped up from under the lab table and walked right over to her jar with a very live frog in it, and dumped it out the open window. She winked at Mina and whispered, "I've been looking for a way to get out of this dissection." She turned to her friends, who Mina recognized earlier from choir, and the other girls followed suit. Three more frogs made a flight to freedom.

"Mr. Pierson! Our frogs have escaped," Melissa said with a very worried expression. "I don't know what happened—we turned our backs, and then they were gone."

"Now, girls, frogs just don't walk off on their own." Mr. Pierson frowned at them and pulled out a key from his pocket, then walked over to the large glass cabinet and unlocked it, looking for another specimen for the girls.

"You're right. Frogs don't walk off, they hop off," Melissa answered innocently.

The whole class erupted into fits of laughter, and Mina used the distraction to slip out the back lab door into the empty hall.

She clutched her head in wonder and tried to make sense of what had happened. *Where's Charlie? Where's my brother?* She began to walk the school halls on tiptoes, calling out her brother's name. *Maybe he appeared in a different classroom, and now he's scared and hiding.*

Room by room she went, storage closet by storage closet. She searched the gym, the locker room, the library, and finally she gave up and sat down in defeat by her locker. She was a terrible Grimm; she had lost her brother again, lost her good friend Nix, who she was sure didn't survive the trip here, and Jared was lost to her. Nothing was easy, and she had a zillion more questions to answer. The final bell rang, and Mina ignored the students coming and going, grabbing their backpacks and leaving for the day. She didn't care. She wasn't going anywhere until she had found her brother.

A pair of white flat shoes stopped by her and gave her leg a little nudge. Mina looked up into Nan's worried face.

Fable

"What's wrong? Are you feeling okay?" Nan leaned down and touched Mina's knee gently. "Do we need to cancel the movie tonight?"

"I'm not in the mood to see a movie," Mina whispered, and tried to ignore her best friend's attempts at conversation.

Nan turned and sat down on the floor next to Mina. "Well, if you don't want to go, I can just take Charlie. He's been dying to see that new movie called *Fable* for weeks now, and I know you didn't really want to see that one anyway. I'm not even sure why, because it's been getting such great reviews."

Mina's head snapped in Nan's direction. "What did you just say?"

"I said that *Fable* has been getting great reviews, and just because you're a sucky sister doesn't mean that I can't be a cool best friend and take *our* little brother to see it." Nan poked Mina in the arm.

"And how long has Charlie been wanting to see it?" Mina's voice quivered in disbelief.

"For-ev-er!" Nan dragged out. "Just last night at your house, he drew me a whole made-up comic strip about it, with a snake, a cute green guy, and a giant. He said I have to take him. Well, okay, he didn't actually *say* I had to take him, but he wrote me a note." She pulled out the paper, and, sure enough, Mina recognized Charlie's scribbles.

Mina lunged sideways and hugged Nan around the neck. "You are awesome as always."

"I know. I know. And one day, you will grow up and become awesome, too. Maybe even as awesome as me," Nan teased, before getting up and putting her backpack on her shoulder. "So, see you at seven, then?"

"Is Brody going?" Mina asked.

"Brody Carmichael? Uh, why would he?" Nan asked, confused.

"Well, aren't he and you...?" Mina gestured with her fingers back and forth between them, and Nan's smile dropped. "Uh, ew. He's your hot boy obsession, not mine. Besides, he's probably at water polo tryouts. But I've got to go run an errand before tonight." Nan waved and headed for the exit, but then turned around and yelled, "If you decide to go watch the practice, bring a napkin to catch your drool."

Mina stood up and laughed at Nan. Could it be that the world had been put back to rights? It sounded like it was. Charlie was home safe and sound, Nan and Brody weren't a fairy-tale item anymore, but where did that leave her and her curse?

She walked slowly to the aquatics building and sneaked into the top row of the bleachers. Sure enough, there was Brody Carmichael, getting ready to do a dive into the water. The tryouts hadn't officially started yet, so the boys, being boys, were roughhousing and trying to dunk each other.

She felt the aluminum bleacher dip as someone sat on the seat next to her. Mina didn't take her eyes off the water for fear that this reality would fade away. Besides, she could tell from the scent of the perfume that it was Mrs. Colbert.

"That was a brave thing you did." She leaned forward and put her folded her hands on her knees.

Mina sighed loudly. "I only made everything worse."

"Did you, now? I thought that this was one of the better outcomes. Of course, it's not the ideal one, but we can live with these consequences."

Mina looked at Mrs. Colbert, and her voice quavered with unshed tears. "I saved my brother, but at what cost? Jared's gone, Nix is gone, and the curse has messed with my friend's memories again. Is there a side effect to all of this tampering? I mean, they're not going to go crazy or anything, right?"

"No, as long as you can hold your reality together and truly believe in it, then they will accept it as well." Mrs. Colbert rocked back and forth on her heels, and seemed really interested in the start of the water polo tryouts. The coach had come in and started giving the men a pep talk.

"Here, you fixed it—I think you should keep it safe." Mina pulled out the seam ripper, which had somehow made it back into her pocket, and handed it to Mrs. Colbert, who fidgeted with the seam ripper.

"Hmm, you should have seen how worried Jared was when he saw you go over to the Fae plane. He found every single piece of the seam ripper and begged us to fix it. It was Ken Wong who finally figured out how it went together. That boy was determined to go after you."

Mina could feel herself getting angry with her teacher, and she couldn't hold back the bitterness in her voice. "You knew, didn't you? You knew why Jared couldn't go back. That his brother wanted to destroy him. You knew all of these reasons, yet you helped him come after me and now he's...he's no longer..."

"Yes, I knew. It's why we kept the young prince in the dark, because one day they might be reunited, and then none of our secrets would longer be safe. Teague is stronger now, and more dangerous. Even the King and Queen can no longer hold him in check."

"Why did they allow it to happen? Why couldn't they control their own son?" Mina felt herself start to tear up again, but she bit the inside of her cheek. She wouldn't be weak anymore.

"Mina, there's something you need to understand about Jared and Teague. This was shortly after, mind you, the Grimm Brothers began their quests to close the gates between the worlds. Teague was engaged to the princess of a neighboring kingdom and almost caused a war when he called it off. It seemed that was his intention all along: to cause a war of mass destruction. To save their son, the Queen and King had the strongest Fae in the land come and try to drive the dark side of Teague out. They did it. They separated his dark personality from his good, but it didn't necessarily split down the middle evenly."

"I'll say," Mina grumbled, remembering how surly Jared could be at times.

"But now that they had split Teague's two halves, they needed to imprison them and keep them far apart from each other so they would never become whole again. So one of the Queen's own handmaidens, a sprite, split the Grimm book that Teague was ever so obsessed with in two and attached each of the two personalities to it, and then sent them to separate planes."

"So are you saying there was never a Jared?" Mina didn't think she could handle this news.

"Oh, no, there was always a Jared. There still is a Jared. He's just one side of Teague."

Mina made a face in disgust. "I don't think I like any part of Teague."

Mrs. Colbert gave Mina a scorching look. "Don't discredit him. After all, there is a small part of Teague that you love and will always love—the Jared side. And if you love him, there's always hope."

"So everything was a trap all along. Teague was just trying to get his other half back over to the Fae plane so he could combine himself again and become even more powerful. All of the quests, everything was just a big fat lie." She yelled out the final word, and it echoed inside the building. A few people stopped to stare at them before they kept on working.

"It's always been his plan, but for it to work, he needed a Grimm to use the Fae book to combine them."

"And I was the only Grimm stupid enough to do it." Mina began to twirl her brown hair around her finger in distraction.

"No, you were the only one brave enough to do it."

"What about my father?" Mina forced the words out and stared at her hands clenched into fists, preparing herself for the worst.

"He, like you, made a deal with the Stiltskin, only his deal was different. He didn't know the real side of Teague and Jared. Your father sought out Temple on this plane and made his own deal. If he died during a quest, he wanted Sara to have a son to replace himself. So, during one of Teague's more deadly attempts at a quest, your father was mortally wounded, and the Stiltskin came to collect. Your father's life for Sara's yet unborn son. He gave the rest of his life willingly, Mina."

Mina's eyes squeezed shut, and her heart filled with pain. "So what did I see on the Fae plane? Who was it I saw released after the Stiltskin died? A ghost?"

Mrs. Colbert reached over and squeezed her hands. "He died in this world, Mina, on the physical plane. I don't think he can come back." She handed her a tissue.

Fable

Mina sniffed and crumpled up the tissue to wipe at her eyes. "Soooo," she stuttered out between crying breaths, "as long as he stays on the Fae plane, he'll live."

Mrs. Colbert picked up the seam ripper and handed it back to her, gently placing it between her hands. "You're not done with this yet, my dear." She smiled softly. "Whether you know it or not. You are one step closer to breaking the curse on your family." She pulled her bag onto her lap and opened it up to pull out a familiar small book. It was the Grimoire.

Mina had been so worried when it didn't travel across to the Fae plane with her, and worried about who would find it. It turned out she didn't have to worry at all. Mina gingerly picked up the notebook and ran her fingers over it. It didn't feel the same. It felt lacking, like it was missing something—Jared.

She opened up the book and found that it was just a book. The cover was still the same, but all of the pages were blank. Her pulse started to quicken, and her hands became clammy.

"What happened? Did I break the curse?"

Mrs. Colbert shook her head. "No."

"Then what—what's going on?"

"You've come farther than any other, and yet you are so young." Her teacher's eyes were sad, and Mina could feel dread creeping over her.

"What's wrong?" Mina asked.

"The Grimoire is just a book, nothing more. It will mimic the Fae book for you, but that is it. It's lost its guardian, and so have you. You've weakened the curse, and now there is only one more thing for you to do to be completely free," Mrs. Colbert whispered sadly.

"Don't. Don't say it." She knew—she could tell just from the way her teacher pitied her that it was going to be bad. And she knew from the intuitive way her heart was breaking that she couldn't do it.

"You said it yourself, Mina. All you have to do to break the curse is kill Teague."

"No…you're wrong," Mina said, trying to convince herself.

"Teague is now more vulnerable than ever. Before he didn't have a weakness. If Jared loves you, then Teague will be feeling those emotions as well. So you have to ask yourself, Wilhelmina Grimm, can you use that to your advantage? You're Jared's greatest weakness, and now you're Teague's. Are you willing to kill Jared to break the curse forever?"

Twenty-Nine

Mrs. Colbert stood up and used her hands to smooth her skirt down and put her bag over her shoulder.

"I don't think I can do it," Mina whispered, and felt her throat start to catch. She had just started to love again, just to lose it. Well, actually, kill it.

Mrs. Colbert leaned down and gently touched Mina's shoulder. "I believe you will do what you have to do. Just trust your instincts and your friends, and maybe, maybe you will survive this tale."

"Why did you have to tell me this? You could have waited, till, like, next week, or next year," she cried out.

Mrs. Colbert scanned the pool and smiled wryly. "There is no time like the present, since the Fae time and your time don't always see eye to eye. Plus, I don't think it will be long before Teague comes for you. After all, he's going to be pretty upset you got away."

Mina sighed and started to pick at a spot on her jeans. This was too much. She hadn't even seen Ever yet. How in the world was she going to tell the pixie that she'd ruined everything? Brought Teague and Jared together, and now she had to kill them both. Was there no bright spot in her future? It seemed like everyone she came in contact with was either hurt, doomed, or dead.

She was so lost in her thoughts that she failed to see what Mrs. Colbert thought was so amusing, since she kept chuckling and laughing.

"Well, that sure is a mighty fine water polo team we have this year, isn't it?" She nudged Mina and pointed.

Mina groaned and felt her cheeks turn red. Her teacher had caught her ogling the guys.

"Especially that new kid, what's his name, Nix, uh, no, that's not right. It's Nick now. I've never seen anyone more acclimated to the water. He may even give Brody a run for his money." She smiled and moved away from the bleachers, her heels making soft clicking noises as she left Mina to her thoughts.

Mina didn't need any other urging. She found herself scanning the water, looking for a green-skinned boy. Oh, what was she thinking? He couldn't possibly have Fae-colored skin here. It only took a moment to see the one young man who was swimming laps around the other athletes. He seemed to be born in the water. His strokes were long and powerful, and he had great stamina and could tread water without breaking a sweat. He actually acted like he had a new lease on life. Well, he did.

It wasn't until he turned around and made eye contact with her that she did actually truly know it was Nix. He was alive and well, and apparently human. His hair was a shocking red color, and his skin was pale white. But his eyes—his eyes were still that brilliant shade of Fae green.

The coach was busy discussing the tryouts with his assistant, and Nix smiled at her and gave her a thumbs-up. Brody used that moment to hit Nix on the back of the head with the ball. Nix's head bounced with the impact, and he turned and dove after Brody, attacking him from beneath and pulling him underwater. Brody's smile dropped from his face as he sucked in a mouth full of water. Brody resurfaced with an impish look on his face and lunged at Nix, pushing his head under the water.

Mina laughed at the boys, who were bonding as only brothers with a love for water could. It looks like Nix had found another family. She couldn't help but think back on what the phoenix had said to her. *Even if I heal him, he will still die on this plane.* It was his Fae self that was dying. By bringing him here, he got a chance to live as a human. A teenager with a future that was much more stable than hers.

Maybe Mina Grimm didn't mess up too badly after all.

Also by
Chanda Hahn

Unfortunate Fairy Tale Series

UnEnchanted

Fairest

Fable

The Iron Butterfly Series

The Iron Butterfly

The Steele Wolf

The Silver Siren (coming soon)

 Chanda Hahn uses her experience as a children's pastor, children's librarian and bookseller to write compelling and popular fiction for teens. She was one of Amazon's top customer favorite authors of 2012 and is an ebook bestseller in five countries.

She was born in Seattle, Washington, grew up in Nebraska, and currently resides in Portland, Oregon with her husband and their twin children.

Visit Chanda Hahn's website to learn more about her other forthcoming books. **www.chandahahn.com**

Acknowledgements

A quick thank you to everyone who helped me with this book.

Stacey Wallace Benefiel, for all of the writing, coffee and Panera dates. If it weren't for you, this book still wouldn't be finished. To my husband Phil, who watched my kids so I could write. To my Beta Readers, Alison Brace, Sadie Mohr, Dominique & Brendon Hamson, Linda Della Volpe & Jennifer Martinez! And of course my editor, who makes me sound smarter than I really am, Joy Sillesen.

CPSIA information can be obtained at www.ICGtesting.com
Printed in the USA
LVOW12s2128020115

421300LV00001B/93/P

9 781491 282021